BEYOND THE CEDAR GATE

ELIZABETH AND THE SAVAGES - UNCHAINED

WENDY J. HATFIELD

Edited by: Goldie Carlon

authorHOUSE®

AuthorHouse™
1663 Liberty Drive
Bloomington, IN 47403
www.authorhouse.com
Phone: 833-262-8899

Published by AuthorHouse   01/14/2022

ISBN: 978-1-6655-4712-3 (sc)
ISBN: 978-1-6655-4711-6 (hc)
ISBN: 978-1-6655-4716-1 (e)

Library of Congress Control Number: 2021924905

Print information available on the last page.

This book is printed on acid-free paper.

CONTENTS

I never saw a wild thing sorry for itself.
A small bird will drop frozen dead
from a bough without ever having felt sorry for itself.
-D.H. Lawrence

This book is dedicated to my twin and my second oldest sister. Without the both of you, Elizabeth and The Savages would never have made it beyond my cedar gate.

The Myth

"She is the seer throughout all the lands.
Her wings touch within and beyond this world.
Her eyes burn like fire from the forgotten souls she
caught wandering in the night.
Haunting the nighttime sky, her voice echoes as it calls out,
'Who… Who do I feed…? Who…?' "

CHAPTER 1

MOMMY HAD JUST GIVEN US OUR MID-MORNING SNACKS. When she opened the door, Sager, Mr. Wienie, and I ran to lay under the tree in the front yard. A gentle breeze was cooling the air, and I felt sleepy. Life was spectacular for three Dachshunds, just like us.

Mr. Wienie nosed the ground as he talked about how great bacon bits would be with lunch. Sager stretched, sat down, and stared at Weinie.

"Is that all you think about?" Sager asked Mr. Wienie as she scratched at her ear.

"Think about what?" Wienie asked, turning in her direction.

"Food." Sager barked back. "Is that all you think about?"

"Why do you always pick on me, Sager? Mommy calls you Mommy's Babysitter, but you're not 'my' babysitter." Mr. Wienie stated adamantly.

"Wienie, I'm the reason you're here. I should have picked your brother instead. Maybe he wouldn't have been such a food hound." Sager snorted.

Mommy and Daddy had rescued my brother, Mr. Wienie when he was five years old. He came all the way from Savanna, Georgia. He was from a puppy mill that had been closed down.

Sager was the first to be saved. She spent her first year alone on the streets in Prosser, Washington. Then a year later, she was moved in and out of different homes because of her temper. She was what Mommy called an 'ankle biter.' She stopped biting after my parents brought her home. Mommy said Sager was just misunderstood. She had to be brave to be all alone on the streets as a puppy.

My parents took Sager with them to pick out my brother a year later. Sager and Mr. Wienie have been arguing for four long years ever since.

Even though they bicker all the time, I know they still love each other. When it's nite-nite time, as Mommy calls it, they always sleep together.

I rolled over to stare at the clouds, wishing for an adventure. I wondered where Daddy was today. You see, I usually travel with him. My Daddy owns a million-dollar crane company. He always says that huge companies worldwide rent his cranes when they need serious construction work done. I'm not sure what serious construction means, but if my Daddy's company does it, it must be good.

He says he gets to play big boy trucks and cranes all day long now. Just like he did when he was a little boy. Only now he gets paid for it, and Mommy, well, she has fun spending the money. My Daddy will tell you whatever makes my Mommy happy makes him happy too. But he always winks when he says that, and I always wonder why?

I lay there in the grass, listening to my siblings squabble at each other, fondly remembering how I came to this family. Mommy and Daddy adopted me when I was four months old. Sager and Mr. Wienie even argued over who got to sniff me first when I was brought home.

That was seven months ago, and it's even worse now. Sager is still as protective as she ever was. She never lets me or Wienie get into trouble. That's why Mommy calls her 'Mommy's Babysitter.'

Oh, my goodness! I haven't even told you my name yet. It's Elizabeth, 'Elizabeth James,' because that's what my Daddy calls me; his middle name is James too. My sister calls me 'Bethy,' but she calls me 'Elizabeth James' when she thinks I'm naughty. Mommy calls me 'Mommy's Little Bit.'

When we're all together, it's like magic in a bottle! Mommy says we are like peas and carrots. By the way, please don't tell her that I don't like peas.

Wait, where was I? Oh, yes, I heard Mommy coming out of the house. She was headed to the backyard again. I wonder what she does back there every day. Is she hiding something? Maybe it's just too dangerous; perhaps that's why we never get to go to the backyard.

Sniffing my way to the cedar gate, I left my siblings going on about who picked who. That's when Mommy came back through the gate and told me to stay in the front yard.

As the gate closed, I looked between Mommy's boots to see what could be so important back there. I had been with Daddy all over the world with his cranes. Together we had seen a great many things. Mommy, Sager, and Mr. Wienie used to travel with him. Now that I'm here, it's my job to keep Daddy company on his long journeys.

Peering through the gate, I wondered again what could possibly be back there. I paced back and forth; my thoughts raced in anticipation. Frustrated, I said aloud, "Why won't Mommy take us to the backyard?"

Then I thought about all the neat places I had been to. What if our backyard was like Area 51 in Nevada? Daddy and I went for a walk there once. We had a great time chasing each other in the grass as we pretended the aliens were going to get us. It was scary but exciting too.

Maybe a giant stuffed black bear would be standing back there. Like the one Daddy and I found in a store window in Missoula, Montana. We named him Smokey Bear. That was a great place. That town even had a park just for dogs. Daddy and I played there for hours. The stories we heard from all the friends we made along the way were so heartwarming.

Now I felt determined and excited to get a better look; I squeezed my eyes shut and pushed my nose through the slats of the gate. I pushed a little more, suddenly, my head slipped through.

I was waiting to be amazed. I kept thinking it had to be fun! Yes! It had to be fun; that's why Mommy comes back here every day.

Slowly I opened my eyes. Really? This is it? I thought to myself, our backyard wasn't anything I hadn't already seen anywhere else before. Grass! With a small stone walkway.

Feeling disappointed, I tried to pull my head back through the slats. I was stuck! The excitement of discovering a new adventure caused me to wiggle too far through the gate, and I couldn't move. I started to panic. I struggled to back up.

Oh no, I thought to myself. How am I going to get out of this one?

I could still hear Sager arguing with Wienie. I started to howl, hoping they could hear me over their bickering. I howled again with all my might. I just kept yelling until I heard Sager ask, "How did you get stuck in there?"

"I'm stuck. How do I get out?" I cried back.

"I'll help you if you give me your afternoon treats." Wienie said slyly.

"Wienie, you never give me your treats when you're stuck in the gate." Growled Sager.

"That's because I deserve all the treats; I do all the yard patrols. I sound the charges signaling when we have company or the mailman is here. I spend most mornings planning the daily maneuvers, and you have the nerve to ask me why I deserve all the treats?" Mr. Wienie grunted.

I thrashed around in the gate, trying to free myself. Wanting Sager and Wienie to stop arguing, I cried out again, "I'm stuck! Guys, help me! Get me out of here before Mommy sees me."

Sager wiggled her head through the gate and licked my face to calm me down. She told Wienie to put his paws on the secret stone to open the gate. I heard him walking away, whispering, "Do I still get your treats?"

"Do it! Wienie, do it now and stop worrying about your stomach." Sager growled again.

Secret stone? My mind raced, and for just a minute, I forgot that I was stuck in the gate.

Sager's eyes sparkled with excitement. I could tell she was holding something back. She licked me on the forehead, pulled her head back through the slats, and followed our brother, Mr. Wienie.

Suddenly I heard beautiful music, and I realized I was free; as the gate was closing, I could smell the scent of a new adventure.

CHAPTER 2

CURIOUS TO SEE THIS SECRET STONE AND HOW IT OPENS the gate, I approached Sager and Wienie. They were quietly whispering to each other. I tried to listen but couldn't make out what was being said. From the look on Sager's face, I could tell she was annoyed with our brother.

Wienie began drawing in the dirt with his paw, barking orders explaining his tactics and strategies like we were headed to battle.

My brother likes to pretend he is a Colonel in the military, leading his troops to his end goal, better known as snack time. He had sketched a picture of Mommy holding him while she fed him treats.

Mr. Wienie stopped drawing, glanced towards the gate, then our brother added a massive pile of rocks to his sketch. The drawing was starting to look very interesting. It kind of resembled our backyard.

I wondered what he was planning this time. Impatiently I asked, "Will one of you please tell me how you made the gate open and where is this secret stone that you talked about?"

Sager replied, "We can't show you right now, but I can tell you how we found the stone."

As Wienie continued to draw in the dirt. I was shaking with excitement and sat down to listen.

Preparing to tell her story, Sager took a deep breath, arranged her feet, and sat back on her haunches.

"A few years ago, when Wienie first came here, we were taking our afternoon nap right here in Mommy's rose garden. Wienie was sound asleep, and I was just drifting off when a tiny creature appeared from a hole in the ground.

The same hole that the stone is covering. It looked almost like a squirrel and kind of like us, only smaller.

When the tiny creature came out of the hole, it was wearing a miner's hat with a light on it. The light from the hat is what caught my eye."

"What's a miner's hat?" I asked.

"Sager can explain that to you later," Wienie interrupted, "listen to the rest of the story, so we can put my plan into action."

Sager laughed, playfully she said, "What you really mean, brother of mine, is that you want the treats you think Mommy is going to give you because you know she will. Then, you are going to fake an injury to keep her busy, so Bethy and I can sneak through the gate."

Slowly raising his voice, Mr. Wienie said, "What's so wrong with that, Sager? Why do you always pick on me?"

"Why do you always want food? I just tell it as I see it, Wienie." Sager replied. "Besides, you're the one that's going to get all the treats anyway."

I barked at both of them. "Stop it! Tell me the rest, then we can go." I could tell Wienie and Sager were both shocked because they stopped arguing and looked at me with surprise. At that moment, I think I surprised myself too. I've never been in command of anything, let alone my siblings and their arguing.

Sager took a deep breath and continued with her story. "The tiny creature sat there for a minute; it seemed to be unsure of what it wanted. I said, 'Hello.' The creature squinted its eyes and chattered something back at me, and then left in a hurry. I was so surprised at what had just happened; I woke Wienie and showed him the hole. He started digging and barking for the tiny creature to come back. That's when we found the stone, and together, we pulled it from the ground."

As I sat there listening to Sager, I became more and more curious. I could feel the excitement building in my body by the minute. I was trying to look around Sager to see the stone, but I couldn't see it, so I sat up to look over Sager's head.

That's when Sager stopped telling me her story and told me I needed to pay attention. Because I would need to know these essential details if we went beyond our cedar gate. She needed me to know everything that she knew so we could be successful.

Sager looked at me, widened her eyes, then said, "Pay attention, Elizabeth; this is the crucial part about the gate. As Wienie and I wiped off the stone, we heard the latch move on the gate. We both looked, and the gate was no longer locked. Wienie and I were confused about how the latched moved on its own. Our brother here told me that day he made it happen because, and I quote Elizabeth, he said, 'I'm cool like that!'"

I chuckled to myself because that is something Mr. Wienie always says, and he always wants snacks for it.

Mr. Wienie excitedly added, "Elizabeth, I stepped on the stone, and the gate opened all the way. I could see that it shocked Sager, so I stepped off the stone. The gate closed. Sager and I looked at each other as I stepped on the stone again. I made the gate open; I told Sager, when are you going to realize that I am, cool like that."

Looking at me, Sager rolled her eyes and said, "Your brother, mister, I'm cool like that, and I were surprised that day. He simply stepped on the stone, and the gate opened. Bethy, it was magical. Beyond our cedar gate is another world. A world that appears to be dark yet feels so inviting. We saw a massive pile of rocks and dirt in the distance. We heard what sounded like rolling thunder, except there wasn't a cloud in the sky. We saw a vast field that seemed to hold the promise of a new adventure. We never made it to the field that day. Because Mommy came out to the porch and called us back."

Mr. Wienie interrupted, saying, "Elizabeth, since that day, we have never been able to go beyond our gate." Then he continued to explain, "The mission could be too dangerous for just one pup alone. One of us needs to keep Mommy busy. Now that there are three of us, maybe we can make this work."

While Wienie finished explaining his plan, I wondered if we should stay home. Daddy had told all of us to stay in the yard before he left, be good while he was gone, and not give Mommy any trouble. But how could we pass this up? How could we not go on this great adventure? Mr. Wienie reassured me that everything would be okay if Sager and I stuck to his plan.

I've been all over this world with Daddy, saving hearts one at a time. But I've never left my own yard without Mommy by my side. Thinking about all the friends I've made in this world, I wondered how many more I could make in that world beyond our cedar gate.

CHAPTER 3

Mr. Wienie went to see where Mommy was and if it was safe for us to leave. When he came back, he was excited because his plan seemed to be coming together. He would soon be in Mommy's lap, snacking on treats.

"Are you two ready?" asked Wienie. "Go to the gate, and I'll step on the stone. Don't forget you both need to be back in an hour."

From the gate, I could see Wienie put both his paws on the stone. The ground shook as the stone slowly disappeared. A mystical tune played as the gate opened. It was a hypnotizing sound, calling me closer, beckoning me onward.

The music made me feel at ease while following Sager through the entrance to this new world beyond the cedar gate.

Sager and I watched as the gate closed, becoming a beautiful wall of flowers. We could no longer see our brother Mr. Wienie.

"Sager, what just happened? Where are we?" I felt a little scared as I asked, "What world is this?"

Sager said, "It's okay, Elizabeth, move closer and stay behind me. Nothing is as it seems in this world."

Remembering what I was thinking this morning while I was looking through the gate, I told Sager I couldn't imagine a world like this could ever exist. Never had I been to a place where it was so surreal and yet so beautiful at the same time.

This new world was dark, but you could still see as if this sun was shining. Birds were singing. As far as the eye could see, there were butterflies and hummingbirds, and I could smell a sweet scent on the wind.

The mystical music that played while the gate opened, now filled my head, making me feel confused. I needed to stop and lay down.

"Elizabeth, are you okay?" I heard Sager say. "Get up! Don't lay down yet."

"Mommy is probably worried about us. We should go back." I whimpered to Sager.

Feeling insecure, I said, "Maybe there was a reason the stone was a secret. We do not belong in this world, Sager."

"Elizabeth! I need you to get to your feet and follow me. Where is the puppy that lives for an adventure that I hear about all the time? Come on! Get to your feet. We only have an hour. Do it for our Daddy." Sager whispered in my ear.

I got to my feet, and my sister kissed my face as she said, "There's my brave little Bethy!"

I followed Sager through what appeared to be grass for this world. It was thick and tall. Sager began to hop up and down as we made our way through the grass. She was trying to see where we were going.

Suddenly she stopped short and turned to look at me with her front paw to her lips. She then pointed and whispered while putting her back foot on my mouth so I couldn't bark. "Shush, I think it's one of those tiny creatures with the miner's hat; if you make any noise, you'll give our location away."

At that moment, I willed myself to not jump in front of my sister and bark. I froze mid-step, waiting. Sager finally motioned for me to follow her. We crawled our way to the top of a small mound of dirt.

We could see the tiny creature moving under the ground. It was headed in our direction, then we both lost sight of its trail.

"Where did it go?" Sager quietly asked.

"I can't see it anymore." I whispered back.

Sager stood up on her hind legs and told me to climb onto her shoulders and look around. Her legs wobbled, we swayed back and forth as I surveyed the land looking for this tiny creature's trail.

"Bethy, you really need to get your nails clipped." Sager giggled, then asked, in all seriousness, "Do you see anything?"

"Stand still, Sager. I'm losing my balance." I replied.

"ELIZABETH!" Sager screamed.

My sister lost her balance, and we both fell. Suddenly we felt the ground quake, then we could hear it. Springing from a hole just in front of us, a tiny creature was coughing and wiping at its face.

Sager, in a panic, pushed me back and said, "Get back. This thing could have fleas, or worse yet! Ticks!"

Then it happened, the tiny creature spoke to us, in a strange accent, yet somehow, we both understood. "I have no such bugs on me! Thank you very much! Could you please back away from my hole?"

Sager looked at the tiny creature and sniffed the air. She was trying to remember where she had heard this accent before.

She sized it up while moving in front of me. She announced, "I'm Mommy's Babysitter, and you had better not harm my sister."

Sager barked so fast and loud, the tiny creature jumped out of its hole while waving its hands as if to surrender. She stopped to listen as the tiny creature started to introduce itself.

"My name is Geordie Jakensen! First thing! Don't ever compare me to a 'Tiny Creature!' I am a 'GOPHER!' I am a very well-traveled GOPHER!" He asserted with a deep voice, "My family originally hails from Scotland! Currently, Betty and I are from 'Calgary, Alberta' to be exact."

I looked at Sager and said, "I can't understand a word that came out of his mouth, do you?"

"I'm not sure Elizabeth, I know I've heard this language before. It's when I was on the road with Daddy and Mommy before you were born. Even before Mr. Wienie came. We were somewhere on the Canadian Border." Sager answered.

"Yes!" Geordie shouted, "I just told you, Betty and I are from Canada! It's taken me 941 Kilometers and three months just to get here. I didn't stop here to be treated like a common tiny creature, as you put it, Sager!"

"Oh no, he didn't; he said her name!" I said in a low whisper. "Oh, no!"

Sager growled and sniffed the air again. She positioned herself to attack. How dare he say her name without a proper introduction! I thought to myself, who does this Geordie Jakensen think he is anyway?

Sager howled. "Hey!" Then she barked wildly, saying, "As long as you know my name, and we know your name. You need to know my sister's name and where she is from too!"

"Where might that be?" Geordie said defiantly as he put his tiny paws on his hips.

Sager stood up on her back legs and cleared her throat. A murder of crows had gathered. They watched in delight as Geordie bounced from one foot to the other, waiting to hear where I was from.

"She is 'Elizabeth' from 'Elizabeth and The Savages Unchained!' She is known and feared by tens of thousands on Facebook!" Sager shouted while turning in a circle to make sure the onlookers were listening. "She takes hearts one at a time! We have come here to conquer your world!" Sager hissed through her teeth as the list went on and on, really working herself up.

Sager finished with a flourish by saying, "All of you need to back away, or 'Elizabeth' will steal your hearts!"

Stepping closer to Sager, I whispered in her ear, "Sager, that's not what I do. I make friends!"

"Elizabeth! I'm trying to scare them. We don't know anything about this gopher, and he could be dangerous. We need to go; we still have to get to the field, and we only have an hour to do this." Sager explained.

"So, you think you're going to steal my heart; nobody takes anything from 'Geordie Jakensen!' He has the 'Cat-Like Speed' of a 'Mongoose.' He moves like 'Dracula,' quiet in the shadows of the night." He bellowed, taunting Sager as he knowingly referred to himself in the third person.

Scared, I howled, "STOP, PLEASE STOP!" Not knowing what a mongoose was, much less a Dracula, I wanted it to stop! "No more, Sager! We are not mean fur babies! Mommy calls us Savages, but none the less we are loving Savages! We do not harm anyone or anything in any world. Ever!"

Just then, another murder of crows swooped the ground, trying to get at Geordie. I leaped forward and covered him with my body, protecting him the best I could from their attacks.

The last thing I remember was Sager's distant-sounding voice, crying my name as she fought the crows off of me.

CHAPTER 4

I COULD HEAR MY NAME BEING CALLED. SAGER WAS IN A panic. She was barking like I had never heard her before. I opened my eyes, she stopped crying, then threw herself at my side and began to whine.

Geordie stood directly over me with a big smile on his face. "Welcome back, little friend maker! You are quite the scrapper." He said gently.

"She is no such thing. She is hurt; what am I going to do? We need to go home. Back away and give my baby sister some space." Sager demanded in a low, frightened voice.

Geordie interrupted Sager, saying, "Elizabeth is trying to speak." Then he asked me. "What are you trying to say, little lady?"

I was trying to tell Sager no. I wanted to stay and continue the journey to the field. I wiggled to my feet and stretched my back. Still feeling a little shaky, Sager pushed me back down, sniffing me and checking for injuries. She checked for feathers in my mouth with her paw.

"Do you still have all your teeth? You didn't swallow a feather, did you? Did those nasty crows bite you?" Sager asked frantically.

She sounded like Mommy at that very moment, scared I was hurt, needing to be taken to a doctor.

"Sager, I'm fine! I'm okay!" I tried to reply.

"What's that? I can't understand you!" Sager yelled in my face.

Placing her ear closer to my mouth. She was yelling in my face as if we were both deaf. I heard Geordie tell Sager, "Maybe if you remove your paw from her mouth, we all can understand her." His Scottish accent was thicker than ever.

Sager bared her teeth at Geordie Jakensen as she removed her paw from my mouth. In her eyes, I could see the fear she was feeling. I needed to show her that I was okay.

I felt terrible because Sager never shows her emotions, least of all fear. She's the one that is always in control. That's why Sager is the babysitter. Mommy always tells her, make sure everyone is okay and no digging.

I used to think that she was a fun sucker. She could suck the fun out of any playful moment that my brother, Mr. Wienie, and I were having.

I thought to myself, I can see right through you, sister! I know that you truly do love me, Sager.

"I'm okay, sister, look!" I said as I sprung to my feet, "Look at me! I can jump!" Geordie celebrated right along with me by jumping up and down in place.

Then Sager yelled. "Hey Geordie, shouldn't you get back in your hole? Before those crows come back and try to make a meal out of you? My baby sister has already saved your life once today."

I wrapped my paws around her neck and whispered, "I love you, sister."

Sager looked into my eyes. I could tell she was trying not to whimper. She said, "What would we do without you. Don't ever do that again! Do you hear me, Elizabeth James?" She was barking in a loud tone now. "I will make sure Mommy makes you take a nap all day, every day! Elizabeth, you will never see the light of day again! No more saving anyone at the cost of your own life! You scared me!" Sager ranted.

"Elizabeth," Geordie said, "you mentioned something about going to a field. The only field I know of in this world is The Field of Mystery and Wonderment. I can help you get there if you let me. It's the very least I can do for you and your babysitter."

Sager bared her teeth at Geordie with a look of disgust and hissed, "We will not need any of your services today, you tiny little creature!"

Sager and Geordie continued to mock each other. "Not this again." I barked. "We have a mission to complete, and any help you can offer Geordie," I said, while looking in Sager's direction, "we are much thankful to receive."

Throwing Sager a look of displeasure, Geordie pointed in the direction we needed to go. He turned to lead the way; calling back over his shoulder, he said, "We need to make it to The Great Stone Ruins before entering The Field of Mystery and Wonderment."

"Where and what are The Great Stone Ruins?" I asked.

"It's a very magical place, where healings and miracles have been witnessed by many in this world." Geordie said with his eyes wide.

"Oh, wow..." Sager said, mocking Geordie. "Just what exactly is the name of this world? Have you ever been to the other side of the flower wall?" She taunted him with many questions as she continued to say. "Come back to my world...."

"Stop it, Sager, and keep moving!" I said, scolding her. I looked back at her and mouthed the words, "We need his help."

Sager sniffed the air and looked the other way while rolling her eyes. Geordie stopped and pointed to the top of the Ruins.

Sager sat up on her back legs to get a better view and said, "It looks like a pile of...." At that moment, I nipped at her heels to make her stop talking, warning her to be kind.

Sager corrected herself with a smirk in her voice and said, "I mean a pile of greatness."

I sat up also to get a better view. Looking for a landmark, I caught the scent of something terrible, and it made my eyes burn.

Sager said to Geordie, "You need to excuse yourself after doing that! We call my brother Mr. Stinky when that happens! You need to learn...."

Deflecting her rude comment back to the smell, I quickly said, "Wait, Sager, that's a different smell!"

Sager lifted her nose again and took a deep breath. Her eyes widened as she leaped in front of me and spoke. "It's a skunk! Back up, or Mommy will be giving us baths for a week."

Geordie jumped in between Sager and me with his hands in the air and said, "Calm down; in this world, it's a privilege to breathe the offensive odor!"

"A privilege? How does one feel privileged by smelling this stench?" Sager asked, while holding her paw to her nose.

As she began to really pinch the end of her nose, it made her sound funny because we couldn't understand what she was saying, and we laughed at her.

Sager stopped and cocked her head to the side and announced, "This is no privilege I care to be a part of, and neither do you, Elizabeth! Friend maker or not! I'm not playing! Mommy will have my hide, plus I'm not going through weeks of baths."

"Hold on! As we approach the hill to The Great Stone Ruins, if we roll in the grass, we will smell as they do, causing them to trust us! We cannot get to The Field of Mystery and Wonderment without first passing through the Ruins." Geordie said assuredly.

I rolled around in the grass, preparing to be accepted. Sager stood watching. She said she was willing to take her chances rather than to have such a foul stench on her beautiful coat as she put it.

CHAPTER 5

THE GREAT STONE RUINS WAS INDEED A MYSTICAL PLACE. It sat high on a hill, with only one broad pathway leading up to the gated entrance. The beautiful tune that played while the gate opened beckoned me once more. A sense of ease and wonderment came upon me, and I was mystified.

Colorful boulders lay in a pile of rubble where it appeared a great hall had once stood. It was an amazing sight and yet sad at the same time. I could see where this world's miracles were once performed and feel the energy and the warmth radiating from within this mystical place. Excited to get a closer look, I took the lead.

"By the way, did I mention the Queen from this world?" Geordie asked.

Sager snatched Geordie from the ground, frustrated she shook him by the neck, then threw him down. Standing with one paw on his chest towering above him, she growled in his face and said, "What Queen are you talking about? You sound as though you forgot on purpose." Then Sager ran to protect me once more, pleading. "We shouldn't trust this mongoose, as he calls himself! Who forgets about a Queen? Who forgets someone as important as this?" Demanded Sager.

"What is a Queen?" I asked, still feeling confused by the stench and the beautiful music that was calling to me.

"No, Elizabeth, who is a Queen? That's how you ask." Sager said to me and continued to explain. "A queen or a king is someone who rules over the land. They can be mean and sometimes not very understanding. Only wanting their very own needs met and at any cost to others."

Geordie interrupted and said, "Not all Sovereigns reign over their Kingdoms the same way; Her Majesty the Queen only wishes peace for this world. I simply omitted a few minor details so as not to scare you the way you are scaring your sister now."

Sager lunged at Geordie again, trying to snatch him up, but he was too quick this time, and he left a long deep scratch on her nose.

Geordie said with his paws in the air, ready for a fight. "Calm down."

Licking the blood from her nose, Sager kicked her back feet one at a time. She was sizing him up. Ready to inflict some pain on Geordie Jakensen when we all heard a loud trumpet.

The musical trumpet sounded like the arrival of someone or something significant. All three of us all turned to see a group of skunks dressed in purple clothing.

Beautiful white feathers adorned their helmets. Their black boots chimed from the silver bells that hung from their ankles. They were carrying a shiny golden barge-like chair. A much larger, well-dressed skunk sat resting in the chair.

The ground shook from their tiny feet, and their voices carried over the wind, "Make way for The Queen." The skunks sang as the trumpets sounded again.

"It's the Queen! Bow quickly!" Geordie instructed us, lining himself up, preparing to greet the Queen.

While grabbing my tail and pulling, Sager said, "Elizabeth James, get up! We do not bow for skunks!"

"We're guests in this land," I reminded her; pulling away, I whispered, "we must be respectful even to sunks."

I sat down next to Geordie and lowered my head. I could see Sager laying down cleaning her front feet, not caring that the Queen had arrived.

Trumpets blared again. Their tiny boots and chiming bells came to a rest.

I lifted my head to see the skunks carefully, setting the shimmering gold barge-like chair on the ground. A pudgy-looking skunk sat at the Queen's feet, looking content as he slowly pawed through a bag sitting on his lap.

Quickly I bowed my head again and listened for the Queen to speak. All that could be heard was the sound of the pudgy skunk muttering to himself as he continued pawing through his bag.

I heard the Queen clear her throat. Then she did it again, only louder this time. Curious, I lifted my head to see what was going on.

The Queen was looking down at the pudgy skunk. Softly she said, "Spencer." He was oblivious that they had even arrived.

With a loud sigh, she tapped her scepter on the arm of her chair, and with an exhausted voice, she loudly repeated his name.

Spencer quickly glanced over his shoulder. His eyes widened as he made eye contact with her. Exasperated, the Queen gestured for him to help her down from the chair.

I felt sorry for him as he struggled to his feet but couldn't move. His feet were tangled in the strap of his bag and the Queen's robe. It caused him to fall to the ground.

All the Queen's guards snickered at poor Spencer as he scrambled to retrieve the contents of his bag that now lay scattered on the ground.

Geordie could see that the Queen was unhappy with Spencer. Quickly he approached the chair and dropped into a deep bow in front of the Queen, exclaiming, "Your Highness, I am Geordie Jakensen. I am of the Jakensen Clan that hails from Scotland. I am your humble servant, and your every wish is my command. With your permission, I have come to travel your land."

The Queen, still sitting in her chair, extended one of her paws to Geordie as a gesture for him to kiss. He took her paw in his and gently pressed his lips against it. Geordie then took a step back while still holding the Queen's paw. He winked at Spencer and helped the Queen grandly descend, which we now know to be her throne.

I looked to see how Sager was taking all this. She had curled her lips as if trying to spit something nasty out of her mouth when Geordie kissed the Queen's paw.

The Queen said, "Whom have you brought with you to this Kingdom of mine? Why does only but one refuse to bow?"

Geordie ushered me forward so I could kiss the Queen's paw. Leaning closer to her, my eyes started to water even more from the foul odor, and it made me cough. Holding my breath, I quickly licked both her paws. I froze, waiting for her to touch the top of my head.

The Queen asked in a loud and commanding voice, "Who are you, and what is your purpose here?"

Geordie stood up and removed his hat, bowing as he said, "Your Royal Highness if I may?"

She nodded and returned to her chair to listen.

Geordie took a deep breath. I could tell he was trying to remember what Sager had said, only he changed it. "She is 'Elizabeth!' 'Saver of all Hearts!' 'Breaker of none!' 'Elizabeth, The Friend Maker!' 'Stranger to none!' "

As he started to shout out another name, I could hear Sager becoming restless. Jumping with all her might, she flew through the air, landing in front of us. Sager arched her back and howled to the sky, declaring....

"She is 'Elizabeth,' and I am none other than 'Mommy's Babysitter' as far as you're concerned!" She told the Queen, barking wildly, "I will not bow to you; I will never kiss your filthy...."

"No! Sister!" I interrupted, "We need to pass through the Ruins to get to the field."

The Queen ordered her men to take us to The Great Stone Ruins. I looked at Sager and said, "What have you gotten us into now with your temper?"

CHAPTER 6

THE QUEEN'S GUARDS CIRCLED US, INSTRUCTING US IN A language that Geordie seemed to understand. One of the guards said, "Ne résistez pas et Suivez-nous."

Looking at Sager, I asked, "What did he say?"

Geordie repeated what was said in a French accent, "Ne résistez pas et Suivez-nous."

"We got that part, Geordie. What does it mean?" Sager asked, sounding really frustrated.

"My French is a little rusty, I believe they said, 'Do not resist and follow us!'" Geordie said with a thick Scottish accent.

"OUI!" Chirped one of the other guards.

Sager quickened her pace and barked in response, "I'll 'OUI' you! Tell them they can...."

Yelling above Sager's voice, I said, "Need I remind you of your recent actions?" I interrupted to save her from further embarrassment with her words. This only frustrated my sister even more, and she began to pant.

The Queen's Guards moved with a sense of urgency. They were rushing us up the pathway! But to what? I thought, what was going to happen once we arrived?

I worried about the others and myself. I could see my sister contemplating an escape. Sager was looking over her shoulder toward the flower wall. She looked at me and then to the path that we had just been on. I shook my head no and continued to follow the guards.

"Do we have time for a nap and maybe a bite to eat?" Asked a very sleepy Geordie.

Sager said, "Wonderful! We have been captured with yet another one who only thinks of his stomach."

"Don't start," I said to her, trying to see in front of the guard leading the way, "we need to try to reason with this Queen, so she will allow us to pass through the Ruins to enter the field."

Looking in Geordie's direction, I noticed he was struggling to keep up with such a fast pace. Dipping my nose down, I flipped him onto my back.

I said, "There, you go, Geordie, take that much-needed nap you requested." I could hear the sleepy tone of his voice as he said, "Wake me when we get there." Closing his eyes, he smiled and then yawned.

Sager repeatedly whined, "Are we there yet?" As we marched into the afternoon.

Suddenly the guards came to an abrupt halt. Sleepy and hungry, I hadn't even realized we had arrived. The Great Stone Ruins now lie before us. They led us to the entrance of the Ruins and ushered us through a door.

We were forced down a long hallway into a big empty room. Once inside, the foul stench was more than I could handle, and I covered my nose with my tail.

Geordie awoke, sputtering and cursing in that strange language the guards were speaking. Sager was complaining again while pinching her nose tight.

The Queen was resting in a vast golden chair. It sat slightly higher than the other chairs in what was once this great hall. We were instructed to kneel before her.

I was afraid Sager would resist again and looked to see if she was kneeling. She only half kneeled, winked at me, saying, "I got this pup!"

A trumpet sounded, calling the court to order. Spencer, the pudgy skunk, appeared beside the Queen, looking very smug.

In a squeaky high-pitched voice, he asked the question again, "Why have you come to this world? Why is it that only two of you kneel?"

Looking from Geordie to Sager, I stood up. Trying to remember how Geordie addressed the Queen.

I bowed my head and, in my most grown-up voice, repeated. "Your Royal Highness, we meant no harm to you or your Kingdom. We come with words of love from our lips. If you will allow us, we only wish to pass through your Great Stone Ruins."

"Our King, Mr. Wienie, has sent us to view your Field of Mystery and Wonderment."

Pausing, I began to think that the Queen might allow us passage to the field if we had royalty in our world too. I decided to wing it with a new plan of making Mr. Wienie the King of our world because he acts like it anyway. Sager lifted her head and snickered. She began to thump the floor with her tail, trying to hold back another snicker.

I continued speaking to the Queen, "King Wienie has instructed us to take no prisoners and to return within the hour."

In a high-pitched voice, Spencer squeaked out, "What is it you wish to know of The Field of Mystery and Wonderment?"

Which caused Sager's ears to perk up as if someone was playing with her favorite squeaky toy.

Frantic, I looked at Sager. Our brother, Mr. Wienie, never mentioned what it was we were supposed to learn. His strategy and tactics only involved delicious snacks and a comfortable nap on Mommy's lap.

Out of the corner of my mouth, I whispered to Sager, "What is it we're supposed to look for?"

Realizing what Wienie had done, Sager started to bark. Not caring for a single second that we were standing in front of a Queen, not to mention her entire Court. "Mr. Wienie! All he cares about is his stomach!" She snarled through clenched teeth.

She howled and howled. "Our brother tricked us! He got his snacks and ours too by sending us to this stinky world!"

Still howling, Sager paced back and forth. It was clear to all in the room she was ready to explode. I knew I wouldn't be able to calm her down.

I looked to Geordie for help. The only way he knew to get her attention was to bite her tail.

Geordie grasped her tail in his tiny claws. Taking careful aim, he attempted to sink his small fangs in. With a look of rage, Sager spun on Geordie, baring her teeth and growling. She hissed, barking loudly, "DON'T EVEN TRY IT, YOU UNDERSIZED GROUNDHOG!"

Geordie threw both hands in the air, and without hesitation, he stroked her nose and whispered, *"My apologies, 'bonnie lass,' I was only trying to help!"*

Geordie looked at the now red, long, deep scratch he had left on her nose earlier this afternoon, and I could see that he felt bad about it.

They stood looking at each other. I could tell he was aware that she was calming down; he continued to rub her nose and ears.

Sager relaxed as if in a trance, his soft fur tickling the inside of her nose. Suddenly she began to sneeze. Uncontrollably, she sneezed over and over again, leaving Geordie covered in a thick slimy mess.

The Queen's Court began to quietly laugh. Spencer wanting to please the Queen, raised his gavel and struck the arm of her golden throne in an attempt to bring order back to the room.

The entire Court burst into laughter. Spencer froze. Dropping his head, the poor pudgy skunk realized his clumsy actions had again disturbed his Queen.

Lifting her paw before she began to speak, the Queen glanced at Spencer as if he had just lost his mind and the whole Court snickered again. She lifted her paw higher to silence the Court and began to speak, "Your King, Mr. Wienie, why would he send you here with no treats?"

Shifting my weight to the other foot, I replied, "Your Royal Highness, it's because King Wienie informed us we would only be gone an hour. Therefore, he said there was no need for treats."

The Queen stated, "We heard you enter this world; because as your cedar gate opened, it triggered our music. We watched as you fought off the crows. We listened as you made friends with your new companion, Geordie Jakensen. Your angry sister was correct when she told you, nothing is as it seems in this world."

The Queen's Court whispered amongst themselves about the series of events that brought us here.

The Queen raised her paw, her voice becoming louder as she continued to speak; "It has not been an hour that you have been in this Kingdom of mine. You and your sister have been here for over a week."

Feeling confused and afraid, I choked back a sob, looking to Sager for answers. My sister always seems to know when I am in distress; she licked my face telling me not to give up yet!

Sager stepped forward and bowed before the Queen. Geordie stood with his slime-covered paw on mine, trying to comfort me. We bowed our heads again.

In a thunderous voice, with all her might, Sager said, "Your Majesty, please forgive my recent actions. Please... allow me to introduce myself.

I hail from another world, just beyond your flower wall. My name is Sager.

Please do not punish my sister, for she only knows love. The King, my sister, is speaking of, is no King. Mr. Wienie is our selfish brother, who thinks only of his appetite. I assure you had he known what we were walking into, he would be here leading the charge." Sager left out the fact that Mr. Wienie despises skunks and delights in chasing them.

The Queen rose and started to speak; Geordie and I lifted our heads to listen.

"I will allow you passage into my Field of Mystery and Wonderment on one condition, that you return with oats from The Mighty Hooved One. I will send my personal guards with you." Then she explained the guards were for our safety.

Remembering what my sister had said before about the queen's and king's, I felt the guards were to keep a watchful eye on us, ensuring her own wants and needs.

While the Queen continued with her own wishes and commands, I was lost in my own thoughts. Should we trust this Queen? Did she really see us when we entered this world? Did she really see us when I had saved Geordie from the Crows?

I could hear Geordie's growling stomach. I, too, was hungry; it had been hours since our last meal. I had not realized Sager was still speaking to The Queen. The only thing I heard the Queen say was, "You will dance for your supper."

The enchanting music that had greeted us at the gate stopped. The Queen's Court began to clap and cheer. Laughter filled the room again, only this time with jeers and snickers. They were taunting the three of us.

Preparing to make an announcement, Spencer loudly clapped his paws together twice. The boisterous room became silent.

"Hear YEE, Hear YEE!" he squeaked. "The guests of 'Her Majesty, Queen Josephine Longwhite the Second, Supreme Ruler of North Finshire of the First Kingdom,' will now step forward and lead the Court in The Meal Dance."

Dance? Did I miss something? I thought. "We are leading a dance?" I asked Sager out loud.

Sager asked for food. I missed her telling the Queen we were hungry. The Queen explained that in this Kingdom, guests must dance before receiving any meal.

The tension that once hung in the room now became a joyous affair. Trays of food were being placed in and around the room amongst members of the Court. I relaxed and watched my sister and Geordie laugh and nuzzle each other. It filled my heart to see their newfound friendship.

Sager kissed the top of Geordie's head and began nudging me to the center of the room. She said, in a sing-song voice, "Let's dance!"

"Wait, wait!" I exclaimed. "Sager, I don't know how to dance."

Sager replied with that special twinkle in her eye, licked my cheek, and said, "I've got this Mommy's Little Bit."

CHAPTER 7

I WOKE TO THE SOUND OF TRUMPETS. GEORDIE WAS LYING on his back between my sister and me. Sager sat up yawning, glanced down at Geordie, and gave him a quick pat on the head. She muttered in a playful voice, "Good morning, my tiny creature friend."

Geordie sprang to his feet, his tiny paws raised in the air. Sager and I began to laugh. He looked like he was ready for a fight. He was swaying back and forth, still half asleep; Geordie mumbled the name Betty as he said, "Nobody touches Geordie Jakensen and his wife!"

Sager licked Geordie on the face and said, "Wake up, little scrapper! It's only us, your friends, Bethy and me, Sager."

Feeling a little embarrassed and relieved, he quickly returned a cheerful, "Good morning, is breakfast ready?"

"Breakfast? How could anyone want food after last night's feast?" I asked.

Geordie stretched and said, "I sure could go for some of that turnip delight. Those skunks really know how to eat. I wonder what was in that carrot cider; I don't remember much after drinking that."

"I don't know much about the vegetables, but that five meat pie was something to howl to the moon about." Sager said while licking her lips.

I sat there in our room, half-listening to Sager and Geordie talk about the meal and remembering how we all danced last night.

I remembered how Sager nudged me to the center of the room as I reminded her that I didn't know how to dance. I could tell she was trying hard to make up for her recent actions.

She told me to copy her as she started clapping and stomping her feet, swaying from side to side, creating a beat. She was trying to stir up the skunks with her newfound excitement, motioning for them to join in. But they only stared at us.

Sager's eyes twinkled as I started to copy her movements. At that moment, I couldn't believe it, Sager was going to have fun! She usually rolls her eyes as she leaves a room, heading for her bed. She nodded her head yes, and told me, that's it sister, just watch me.

When she started to half sing and speak to the skunks, I worried about what she would sing, knowing how my sister could be. Despite the skunk's lack of enthusiasm, Sager began singing and dancing as I did my best to dance alongside her.

I could see Geordie on the sideline, clapping his hands in time to Sager's beat. He was having a great time. I motioned for him to join us.

Geordie two-stepped his way across the dance floor, stumbling a few times; he yelled for someone named Betty and for her to bring him another round.

The Queen appeared rosy-cheeked and very taken with Geordie's dancing, and it wasn't long after that that she too joined in. The younger skunks began to clap; some of them even joined in the dance.

I could hear "Hee Haw" coming from every direction of the room. Sager jumped into the crowd, landing on a few of the skunks' backs.

She surfed the crowd as they spun her around and around. The skunks' tails shook in the air as they danced, touching noses with each other it was a strange little dance, but none the less we were all having fun, including the Queen.

I could tell Sager was enjoying being in control. It was clear the Queen was very pleased with us. She nodded to Spencer and then to the table that had been prepared for us to eat. Spencer escorted us to a sizable, lavishly set table. It was covered with various sorts of meats and sauces. It was the kind of meal my brother Mr. Wienie would howl endlessly to the moon about.

As Sager and I sat eating, I could see Geordie, the Queen, and her personal Guards, Marcel and Andre. They were lifting their tiny goblets in the air, toasting each other.

However, only one of the guards raised his cup to celebrate, and I wondered why Andre had not?

Geordie, too, it seemed, was enjoying his newfound friends. I felt terrible for snapping at Sager yesterday. It warmed my heart to see her letting go, trusting enough in her own strength to be herself amongst these strangers.

I thought of my Daddy and all the friends we made while on the road selling cranes this past year. I never imagined I would make so many more here in this world beyond our cedar gate. Excited, I said aloud, "Right here in our own backyard." Then I paused, thinking, are we still in the backyard?

Suddenly a guard appeared in the doorway to our room, pulling me back from my memories. He said, "La Reine souhaite vous parler." Then he quickly walked away.

Geordie placed his paw on mine and translated what the guard said. He told me the Queen wanted to speak with us.

Together, we went down the hallway back to the great room where the Queen sat with her Court. On the floor at her feet were two small backpacks and a bota bag full of carrot cider.

Kneeling before the Queen, Geordie said, "Your Majesty has requested to speak with us; how may we be of service?"

The Queen was whispering to the pudgy skunk with the squeaky voice. Geordie twisted his hat in his hands as he waited.

Unsure if she heard him, he repeated, "Your Majesty has requested to speak with us." The pudgy skunk held up his paw to silence Geordie as he continued to listen to the Queen.

Sager began to pant when the pudgy skunk started to whisper back to the Queen. She tried not to fidget, and she said, "How long is this going to take?"

Waiting for the Queen to acknowledge Geordie, my thoughts drifted to Mr. Wienie. For a second, wishing, it was me in Mommy's lap, having my tummy rubbed while she fed me yummy snacks. Hoping Mommy wasn't worried and calling for us. I wondered again how long we have really been here.

The Queen lifted her scepter to Geordie's forehead, allowing him to rise. Geordie rose as she spoke, "As you can see, these backpacks are filled with apples as an offering to The Mighty Hooved One. You must not lose any along the way, lest The Mighty Hooved One will know. The guards will show you what to do with the carrot cider in the bota bag. You are to fill each backpack full of oats and return with them."

The Queen's voice became more serious. She continued on with, "Many brave skunks have attempted this journey, very few have been successful. I am sending my personal guards with you, known throughout the Three Kingdoms in this world, as the best Warrior Skunks.

As her voice carried across the once magnificent great hall, she said, lifting her left paw, "For your safety, I offer you, Marcel of the Third Kingdom."

With a proud smile beaming, he addressed the cheering crowd, then bowed to the Queen.

Turning to her right, she announced, "Andre of the Second Kingdom."

Andre quickly bowed to the Queen and stood looking over the crowd. I could see the open wounds on his nose from his most recent battle. The onlookers had not cheered for him. Whispers of his conquests could be heard as the room became quiet.

Then Marcel and Andre bowed and presented their swords to us. Sager sniffed at the top of their heads; she enjoyed the attention as if she was also royalty. Marcel and Andre stepped back beside the Queen as she continued to speak. "The Wagon Masters will take your backpacks and load them onto a wagon with plenty of provisions for your journey. I have appointed two of my personal footmen to you. They will pull the wagon and attend to your needs. Marcel and Andre will lead the way, providing safe passage."

Still feeling overwhelmed, I looked to Sager and then back at Geordie. They each had a look of bewilderment on their face. Sager whispered to me, "We can still head home if you want to."

I wondered again, what had our brother really sent us here for? Was this journey to The Mighty Hooved One worth it just to see their Field of Mystery and Wonderment? Should we walk away from this adventure? Remembering the excitement of all the new places and people Daddy and I would meet while traveling made my heart pump faster. Recalling the way, I was always amazed by what we found when we would stop. The stories we told from our adventures were happy and exciting times.

Helping to bring awareness to those in need was such a great feeling. This was like being with Daddy again. I needed to let go of my fears and be that adventurous fun-seeking puppy that I was before I came to this world. I now knew we definitely had to do it.

CHAPTER 8

THE QUEEN'S FOOTMEN WERE WAITING BY AN OVERLOADED wagon just as she promised. Looking back towards the direction of the flower wall, I hoped Mommy wasn't worried and calling for us. I thought to myself, soon, Mommy! Soon we will be home. Real soon!

The streets were lined with the Queen's Court, cheering and waving us on. Andre and Marcel led the way as the two Footmen pulled Geordie and our provisions in the wagon.

The well-wishers' voices faded into the distance as we descended down the hill into the valley. I could see that a small brook connected all Three Kingdoms together.

Stopping to take in the view of the vast field before me, I could see the pathway ahead. It was overgrown and trailed off into the darkness of this Kingdom, hiding its many mysteries in the lush tall grass.

The lights radiating from The Great Stone Ruins sparkled on the heavily dew-laden trees just to the west in the Second Kingdom. The sweet smell of wildflowers filled the air, and I could now hear the soft babble of the brook.

A brilliant light pointing to the sky was coming from the Third Kingdom just off to the east. I now understood why Sager and Mr. Wienie were so intrigued and mystified by this world.

Sager sniffed the ground as we walked; occasionally stopping along the way, she was trying to get every last scent of this world all at once. I could tell she was enjoying the adventure.

My sister finally stopped being so protective of me. I smiled and thought to myself, could it be that now she would let me grow up a little?

I asked her if she and Mr. Wienie had made it this far the day they removed the stone from the ground.

With excitement building in her voice, she recalled that day, "We only saw the pile of rubble and heard the thunder off in the distance before Mommy called us back. Wienie and I vowed to come back someday. I never dreamed it would be with a new baby sister." She said in a playful tone.

I wondered aloud, asking Sager, "Why would they call this field 'The Field of Mystery and Wonderment?'" Jumping up and down over the grass, trying to get a better view, I said, "What makes this place so mysterious and wonderful, anyway, or is that just the name they gave this field?"

"Elizabeth, this whole world is a mystery of wonderment. We will just have to take this adventure one step at a time." Sager replied, still sounding upbeat.

Suddenly I remembered what our brother, Mr. Wienie said before we left our yard, he said, 'We saw a vast field that seemed to hold the promise of a new adventure.' Then I made the mistake of actually saying it aloud.

Sager froze; mid-step, she sat down and began to rant, emphasizing places and names. She stated, "Here we are off to haul apples for this 'Big Hooved One.' Do you call hauling apples an adventure? And the 'King,' our 'brother,' is most likely laying on his back eating bacon treats and probably ours too. And has completely forgotten to even check to see if we're at the front door waiting for him. Let alone worrying!"

A light breeze moved the tall grass and seemed to tickle Sager's hind leg at that moment. As Sager spun on her heel to see what was tickling her leg, I decided to lay down on the pathway to chew the bark off of a stick.

I needed to keep myself from laughing out loud. But I also wanted to enjoy more of the rant I knew was about to happen.

Sager bulldozing through the grass bellowed, "What is tickling me?" Then continued her rant with, "I bet Wienie doesn't even know we've been gone longer than an hour." She finished up with, "And let me tell you this. When we get back home. Our brother, 'King Wienie,' as you put it to 'Miss Thang'-'The Queen,' is really going to get it, and he'll wish he really WAS an 'Emperor' off on his own 'adventure' by the time I'm done with him."

Wow! Just moments before, my sister had been in such a playful mood, and it seemed to me that if Mr. Wienie was in front of us right now, she would run his tail-fur backwards.

She stood up, snapping at the air. Full-on into her rant, I licked Sager in the face hoping to calm her down. She became more and more upset with every statement of what she thought we had been through and what we still needed to do before we could go home.

I pulled Sager by the tail, teasing her, saying, "There's nothing 'Big' about The Mighty Hooved One. We're just taking him some apples, picking up some oats, for 'Miss Thang' as you put it, and then we'll go home. Let's chill out and try to have some fun."

Too late, I realized I shouldn't have brought up our brother. I tried to make my sister laugh; I imitated Spencer in a squeaky high-pitched voice and ranted a bit about the skunks' aroma back at her.

Sager laughingly rolled her eyes, looked at me, and said, "Do you have to be so dramatic? Come on, let's go."

As we followed behind the wagon, I could see Marcel and Andre's tails above the tall grass ahead of us in the distance. Disappearing and reappearing in different locations as they checked and secured the pathway for danger.

The two Footmen pressed forward. Leading us onward to The Mighty Hooved One. The monotonous rickety sound of the wagon caused Geordie to yawn. Making himself comfortable, he propped his arms over his head, stretched, and closed his eyes. Easily falling asleep.

The broad pathway abruptly ended as we came upon a small clearing in the thick grass. The path we had been traveling on turned into three separate small trails. It was clear two of the trails were used quite often. The other one seemed ominously overgrown. I could see very few ever ventured that way. The Footmen stopped, unsure of the direction we were to take.

Sager and I needed a moment to stand upwind from the scent of these skunks. After traveling slowly into the field along the path throughout the day, we needed a break.

We went to the front of the wagon; the two Footmen were rummaging through the cart while we were waiting for Marcel and Andre to return.

The Footmen were dressed vastly different than the soldiers who had led us to The Great Stone Ruins. They weren't wearing any shoes; their helmets were made of unadorned leather, and they wore simple aprons with big pockets. Not at all like the beautifully ornate purple uniforms that the skunks who carried the Queen wore.

It was evident the way he shouted out orders; the older skunk was in charge. The tone of his voice caused the much younger skunk to be clumsy and nervous. Wearing a much too-large helmet, the younger skunk constantly tripped over his paws.

As the younger skunk adjusted his helmet yet again. Sager said, "Excuse me, where do these trails lead to?"

I laughed to myself because the sound of Sager's voice startled the younger skunk. His helmet fell forward, covering his eyes and banging the bridge of his nose.

Embarrassed, he quickly pushed the helmet back into place, looked up, and pointed as he answered. "This clearing is called 'Resting Flat Rock.' The trail in the middle leads to The Mighty Hooved One."

At that moment, Sager and I turned to look in the direction he was referring to, and we heard a wet choking sound.

We turned back to see the older skunk removing the chinstrap from between the younger skunk's front teeth, saying, "It is most likely the one we will use." The older skunk was rough as he pulled the helmet away from the younger skunk and threw it in the wagon.

The younger skunk sighed heavily and sat down with his back to the rest of us to rub at his feet as he introduced himself. He said, "Hi, I'm Louie; my friends call me Lou. My family is new to the Queen's Court. He pointed over his shoulder to the older skunk and said, "This here is Stan."

Louie turned to face us as he continued to talk and rub at both of his feet, "I have never been to see The Mighty Hooved One. I used to work alongside my father as a Wagon Master. They are the ones that load the wagons for long journeys."

Evidently, Louie's feet were feeling better; because he excitedly jumped to the side of the wagon, pointing to the trail leading to the east. "Life is much different here than where I come from."

Stan looked irritated at Louie's constant chatter and moving around. This time, however, he couldn't tug at his helmet.

"My family and I just moved here from the Third Kingdom. My mother insisted I join the Queen's service. She thinks I will have a promising future here." Louie added as he did a backflip mid-jump to the ground. Hearing and seeing this Stan, snorted and mumbled under his breath. It was clear that Stan was unamused by Louie's never-ending antics.

Louie didn't have the same accent as the other skunks. He sounded and looked similar to Marcel. Their coats were spotted with white patches, while the others had one wide white stripe that ran from their noses to the tips of their tails.

"Where does this trail lead to?" Sager asked again as she sniffed the overgrown trail to the west.

Stan fearfully searched the sky then, with purpose, began loudly rearranging the wagon load. It was clear he didn't want to answer any questions about the ominous trail. He then gruffly scolded Louie, telling him to get back to work. I began to wonder what exactly it was that Stan seemed so afraid of down that trail.

Sager asked, "Can you hear that? What is that noise?" Cocking my head to the side, I listened. I could hear a low buzzing sound. Curious, I jumped onto the wagon to get a better look at the area.

The buzzing noise was becoming louder. I scanned the field and saw a swarm of bees surrounding Andre.

He was swinging his sword in the air, jumping forward and then jumping back. Confident with each and every step as he thrust his tiny sword forward and then protected himself with his shield.

Seeing Andre do this reminded me of a movie we once watched with Mommy where they were sword fighting.

Breathless Marcel appeared through the grass; he told us all to stay with the wagon, then scampered away.

Unaware we had stopped, Geordie sleepily sat up, rubbed his eyes, and wanted to know if we were there yet. Sager motioned for him to get down, so she could explain what was going on.

I watched as Marcel popped up out of the tall grass just a few yards from Andre. He made a squeal from the back of his throat to get Andre's attention.

Even though the swarm was growing, Andre turned and raised his head above the grass; he locked eyes with Marcel, who motioned for Andre to follow him eastward.

Andre responded with a nod and then continued to fight, thrusting and pushing the large swarm in the direction Marcel had indicated.

The Queen had called them her best Warrior Skunks known throughout the Three Kingdoms. I now understood why she referred to them this way after watching Marcel and Andre battle the giant swarm together, like a finely tuned machine. They were fearless. I was in awe.

CHAPTER 9

STAN AND LOUIE BEGAN HANDING OUT TRAYS OF FOOD. As I reached for mine, Geordie said, "Save the turnip delight for me." Thirsty, he popped the cork on a jug of carrot cider and took a long swig.

With a big sigh, Sager sat down. I could tell she was resisting the urge to complain. She quickly turned her attention to the tray placed before her and began to eat.

I finished my food and laid down beside the wagon. Thinking about Andre, I wondered how one becomes a Warrior.

Geordie was telling stories to Louie and Stan when Andre and Marcel returned. They were dirty and covered with swollen red welts.

As he reached for the jug from Geordie, Marcel said, "We must prepare the wagon to make way."

Andre explained we were in the land of the Cicada Hornets. He said, "We led them to the edge of the Third Kingdom. We fought them the best we could, and we were finally able to escape, for now. We should be okay here, but none of the trails are safe right now."

Struggling to catch his breath, Marcel interrupted, "The buzzing sound you are hearing is to intimidate and discourage predators."

He continued with, "Skunks enjoy the spring weather here. It's when the Cicada Hornet's larvae are in abundance; they make for a fantastic feast in the dark of the moon." Stan licked at his lips in agreeance.

Geordie interjected in a rather knowing voice, "Cicada Female Hornets will use their stingers to protect themselves. The buzzing sound you are hearing is coming from the males. They guard and defend their nests in the ground."

His eyes grew more prominent as he stood on his toes. "If stung in the mouth by the females, reactions to their venom could become lethal." He said, falling to the ground grasping his throat, pretending to be stung.

Turning away from Geordie's theatrics, Andre motioned to Marcel, they began discussing a different route. I heard Andre state, "If we take that trail, it will take an extra day."

Sager and I looked at each other. We both knew we didn't have an extra day. We had already been here for too long.

She told me she was worried that Mommy would be looking and calling for us. We left Geordie, still pretending to be stung, all the while he continued to tug at the jug of carrot cider. Sager and I moved closer to the Queen's Guards to hear the plan.

Andre and Marcel were looking at a map and pointing; Marcel suggested different routes with the least amount of danger along the way. I saw from the map, it resembled this field and the clearing where we now stood, Resting Flat Rock. It had pictures of the skunks feasting on the hornet's larva.

The Three Kingdoms were shown on the map with numbers, with one pathway leading from The Great Stone Ruins.

To the south, just outside the Three Kingdoms, a grove of trees lined a small creek with an old barn. A U shape had been drawn, indicating where we could find The Mighty Hooved One.

Pointing to a smaller trail to the west, Andre said, "If we go this way into my Kingdom, we can pass through The Marsh-Lands; the cattails will shield us in the night."

He had pointed to a giant oak tree that towered above a small pond with cattails. On the tree, I could see the name Georgia had been written.

We could hear the Cicada Hornets returning to their lands as Marcel rolled his map to put it away. Andre suddenly interrupted and explained, "The hornets' lands span throughout the three trails. We have to wait until morning to pass through when they are still in the ground."

Geordie coughed to get our attention. I looked as he lifted his head to see if anyone was watching. Jumping to his feet, he expressed he was very experienced with these hornets by saying, "We don't have to find another way!" Swaying around and struggling to stand upright, he declared, "All we have to do is wait!" He said, sounding like a trumpet announcing good news.

We all looked in Geordie's direction. Andre said, "We should take that jug away from him."

Sager flipped Geordie onto her back with her nose so he could be seen and heard.

With a very serious voice this time, Geordie said, "Cicada Hornets return to their nests in the ground once the sun sets." Then he lifted his paws above his head as if to celebrate.

"The sun never rises or sets here in this world, so how is that going to help us?" Sager asked.

Geordie pulled his sleeve back, looked at his watch, and then to the sky, and said, "By Calgary, Alberta time, the sun should be setting in about 30 minutes. If we wait for them to go into the ground, we should be able to pass through unharmed."

Sager whispered to me, "How long have we really been here? It doesn't really feel like it's been over a week, does it?"

I touched her paw; then she licked my face. "As long as we stay together, Elizabeth," she said and then looked away, hiding her fear. She was unable to finish her statement.

Marcel and Andre agreed to wait and continue through The Marsh-Lands into the Second kingdom, seeing that Geordie was sincere this time.

Louie and Stan loudly whispered the name I had seen on the map. They seemed afraid and mystified all at the same time. Marcel called to them to quickly make a small fire so they could tend to his wounds. I watched as the busy skunks helped each other, all of them except for one.

Andre set off by himself, staring into the field as if looking at ghosts. As I approached, I could tell he was sad. I hesitated, not knowing what to say to him. I picked up a small bowl of fresh water and took it to him. I asked him if he was thirsty, he didn't respond. I took a few more steps and thanked him for keeping us safe.

In a deep raspy voice, Andre replied, "It's what Warriors' do."

I said back to him, "You shouldn't be by yourself. Come and sit with us by the fire. We can help you with your wounds."

Marcel, Stan, and Louie were surprised that I spoke to Andre, and he answered back. I soon learned that no one ever dared to approach Andre. He never talked to anyone, only giving information and answering questions when necessary or directly to the Queen.

The awkward silence was making me uncomfortable, and I blurted out, "How does someone become a Warrior?"

"Why do you wish to know?" Andre asked, looking right through me. He continued as if he was hypnotized, not giving me a chance to answer.

"A Warrior goes to battle, inflicting pain to those in his path. However, a great Warrior will look at the battle and fix it without ever raising a sword. Many will never understand this until it's too late. Not every battle has to be won. In every war, someone must win, and someone must lose. Sometimes you are winning by losing."

I had to lose to win, I thought to myself. Andre had talked in circles, and I wondered if the red spots had made him feverish. I felt sorry for him and wondered how such a brave Warrior could be so sad.

Then Andre turned and looked at me, his eyes holding a memory causing him pain. Trying to comfort him, I asked, "Why do you sit by yourself?"

Turning his attention to the field once more, he replied, "I sit with the memory of those before me. I feel the loneliness for the pain I have caused to those in my path."

I was getting nowhere fast with Andre. I wanted to lighten his heart, but how? Then I remembered Mommy once saying, 'Time spent with someone and listening is the best way to heal a broken heart.' So, I sat quietly.

A few minutes passed, then Andre said, "Many speak of who you are. How can you be so brave without first seeing the faces of pain or death? How do you travel the many kingdoms with no shield or weapon to wield? I've heard you take over hearts one at a time and leave no wounds, friend to all, and a stranger to none. How do you conquer with only a smile?"

Without even taking a breath, I smiled and said the only word that came to my mind. "Love."

Andre turned and faced me as if he was seeing me for the first time.

CHAPTER 10

THE LOW BUZZING SOUND HAD COME TO A STOP. WE COULD now pass through the Cicada Hornets lands into the Second Kingdom. Soon we would be to The Mighty Hooved One, exchange the apples for oats, fill our bags and return.

Geordie had climbed to the top of the wagon to get a better view along the way. Andre went ahead to check the new trail while Marcel held back, ensuring the hornets would not follow us. Before he went ahead of us to secure the trail, Andre told us it would take a few hours to get to the edge of The Marsh-Lands if we hurried. He also instructed Stan and Louie to wait for his signal before crossing the creek into the cattails.

The Great Stone Ruins' lights shimmered on the small trail leading us to Andre's Kingdom. Louie and Stan began whispering between themselves as they tugged the heavy wagon through the overgrown trail. I could hear them talking about Georgia, the name I had seen on the map.

I asked Sager if she had seen the name as well. She said she had, and then she wondered out loud who this Georgia was.

Hearing what Sager had asked, Stan replied with a look of horror on his face and frightened tone as he repeated the stories from long ago,

"She is the seer throughout all the lands. Her wings touch within and beyond this world. Her eyes burn like fire from the forgotten souls she caught wandering in the night. Haunting the nighttime sky, her voice echoes as it calls out, 'Who... Who do I feed...? Who...?' "

Stan was now whispering and looking to the sky as if this Georgia was nearby. "We should not be out here." He said as he shielded his head.

Louie said, "I have never been this close to the Second Kingdom; very few have and lived to tell the tales of Georgia.

Feeling a little afraid, I moved closer to Sager. I asked, "Does she live in that tree that's on the map?"

Startled by a noise that was fast approaching from behind us, Marcel appeared and answered, "No, she is a myth, a story the elders tell to scare children to make them stay in their beds."

Marcel slowed his pace as he approached the wagon, he was cutting away at the trail. When I asked, "What's a myth?"

"A myth is a make-believe story or an idea that is believed by many but is not true." Marcel replied as he approached us.

Sager asked suspiciously, "Then why do Stan and Louie scare us with their story as if they know differently?"

Marcel replied in a harsh voice, "It's just a name. They should concern themselves with getting this wagon to the Marsh-Lands instead of whispering like scared children in their beds."

Marcel continued to cut away at the tall grass as he took the lead, calling out to Louie and Stan to move quickly. We marched into the night until the trail had become muddy, with jagged rocks. Slowing the wagon down, making everyone's feet sink into the thick heavy mud.

Louie and Stan struggled as they heaved and shoved the wagon onward. It creaked and moaned as the wheels were forced slowly onward.

Sager started to hum. I could tell she was trying to amuse herself as we slowly followed. I asked her what she had thought about Stan and Louie's stories. She said, "I don't want to cross the creek."

Sager didn't answer my question, and I now knew why she was humming. She hated to get wet. She always runs and hides when Mommy announces bath time. Just the thought of her paw being dipped into the water made her cringe.

"Sager, what do you think about Stan and Louie's story?" I asked again, trying to get her mind off the creek. She only stared into the tall grass with a look of uncertainty on her face.

Geordie sat up, still half asleep, and started digging around. He was looking for another jug of carrot cider.

I told Geordie the scary bedtime stories that Stan and Louie had whispered to us. He stopped rummaging through the sacks and swiftly came to the back of the wagon. He peered to the sky and said, "Georgia?" Quickly he held his tiny paws to his mouth as if to take back the name.

I sucked in my breath as I, too, looked to the sky. It wasn't a myth that was only whispered to the restless skunk children. My heart raced because we were headed right to the tree where Georgia lived.

Stan and Louie hoisted the wagon over a huge rock and suddenly lost control; it slammed to the ground with a loud bang. It was so loud I jumped. The wagon now lay in a heap on its side.

Geordie was thrown to the ground along with the backpacks, and all our provisions were scattered throughout the tall grass. The remaining jugs of cider were crushed under the wagon.

Sager and I rushed to help Geordie to his feet. "Betty! What a ride!" That was all Geordie could muster as we helped him up.

Unable to free the wagon. Marcel told Stan and Louie to gather the food. We found the backpacks while Geordie quickly retrieved the bota bag from the wagon.

Remembering that the Queen said we would need the carrot cider later, Geordie resisted the urge to have a drink.

Marcel reminded us not to lose any apples, repeating as the Queen had said, 'Lest The Mighty Hooved One should know.'

The light from the Ruins faded as we left the wagon behind. The babbling creek was becoming louder as we pushed on into the darkness.

The outline of the old tree could be seen now on the skyline. I looked to make sure Georgia wasn't there. Marcel, Stan, and Louie were cutting away at the path.

It was clear we were entering into the Marsh-Lands. The trail became slick; we climbed over steep moss-covered rocks leading to the bank of the creek. We had arrived.

Geordie knelt before the rushing water to quench his thirst. Stan and Louie began making funny little noises into the air, signaling to Andre that we were ready to cross the creek.

As we waited to hear back from Andre, Marcel instructed us how to cross the creek; he said, "The Footmen will go first. Watch how they cross through the water. You need to be careful of the current and swim towards them. They will help you over the rocks once you reach the other bank."

Andre had signaled back; it was time to cross the creek. We could see he had lit a small fire and was waiting for us. Sager began to pace back and forth as we watched Stan and Louie pass through the swift water. They were skilled and made it look easy.

They carried the food and all our provisions on their backs. Marcel turned and asked who wanted to go next. While backing away from the water, Sager nervously stated, "I've already had my bath this week."

Hesitating, she sat down then asked, "Is there a better place to cross this creek? Maybe one without water?"

Geordie realized Sager was scared. He hopped on her back and began rubbing her ears, helping her to relax. He said, "I am right here with you, ' *bonnie lass.*' We will take it one step at a time." Geordie continued to rub Sager's ears as he coaxed her into the water step by step.

Soon Sager was swimming into the current, and I could hear Geordie as he sang a silly little tune to keep my sisters mind off the water. *"Oh, I love to go swimming with my bow-legged Betty and swim…."*

I didn't hear the whole song that Geordie sang. But it had to do with Betty and her being bow-legged and a current that ran downstream.

Sager laughed at Geordie's song. She sounded more at ease as she continued to paddle across the creek. But I did hear him say, soon, we will warm up by the fire with a tray of delicious snacks.

I watched as Stan and Louie helped Sager and Geordie over the rocks and onto the bank. Marcel helped me into the water, it was cold, and the current was strong. He stayed beside me, guiding the way through the water. The creek was wide, and it was hard to see.

Andre greeted us at the edge of the bank. He gestured for us to join Sager and Geordie. They were resting along with Stan and Louie.

They had prepared a small snack and were all enjoying the comfort of the bright glow from the tiny fire.

The creek had been cold. I shivered while I warmed myself next to the fire. Sager came and sat next to me. I leaned against her, noticing she was still wet. She kissed the top of my head and continued to eat from her tray.

The cattails swayed in a gentle breeze that carried an unfamiliar scent. Sager stopped eating and lifted her head into the breeze to recall a memory.

Then we heard the thunder. It was rolling and coming from the ground. The ground shook again. Behind it, a thick cloud of dust hung in the air. It was hard to see. Stan and Louie scattered and took cover in the tall grass.

I looked to the sky; I thought I saw something moving in the shadows. We could still hear Stan and Louie scurrying around in the tall grass, trying to hide. They were chanting Georgia's name and wishing they were home.

Feeling afraid, I pressed against Sager as Geordie clung to her front leg. The dust had settled now; Andre and Marcel jumped to their feet, looking at each other.

Andre said, "The Mighty Hooved One knows we are here. He's waiting for us. We must go, lest we keep him waiting."

Stan and Louie found their way through the darkness back to the fire. They were reluctant to press on and wished aloud to return to the safety of The Great Stone Ruins.

Marcel quickly scolded them in a very harsh tone stating again, "Georgia is only a myth. She has never been seen."

Andre sat down and stared into the darkness again with a heavy sigh. He said, "She is no myth, for I have seen this Georgia." I could hear the sadness in his voice again.

Andre began to repeat the bedtime stories of Georgia. Geordie covered his mouth and squeezed his eyes shut. Stan began to look to the sky and take cover as if she would magically appear right in front of them just by speaking her name.

Andre lowered his voice and said, "It was late spring. The grass was barely over our backs. We had traveled through the cattails into the Marsh-Lands to harvest the angelica plant.

My mother used the leaves and the roots to make salves and teas for my younger brother Martin. He was much smaller than the rest of us and had a breathing problem. She said it would also ward off any evil spirits should they be near."

Andre paused, gazing into the fire. Then he closed his eyes and began to whisper. We could barely hear him as he spoke. "The grass, it just wasn't tall enough yet. We didn't know the journey would be so dangerous."

He repeated several times about the grass not being tall enough; he was now talking to himself as if we were not there. Geordie jerked, looking over his shoulder, pulling Andre back to his story.

Andre took a deep breath and continued, "My brother and sisters and I played while mother gathered herbs throughout the day. A breeze from the south indicated that it was time to head home. It was starting to get cold, and soon the dark of the moon would be upon us. Mother led us back to the cattails, told us to wait until she signaled to cross again into the grass. Martin began to wheeze from the steep climb. My sisters went ahead into the grass. I picked Martin up to carry him, and he wiggled free. My brother became afraid and ran back into the cattails. Reaching for him, I heard a whooshing sound from above. Silently a large feathered, fiery-eyed creature landed behind Martin. He was still trying to catch his breath. I could see into the mysterious red eyes of this creature as it gazed upon my brother. Unable to catch his breath, Martin collapsed. The creature stretched its wings to take flight, picking my brother up in her large talons. The creature said, 'I've got you.' Then she disappeared into the shadows of the night with my precious brother."

CHAPTER 11

WE ALL GAPED AT ANDRE, WAITING TO HEAR IF HE EVER saw his brother again. Andre looked to the sky, and with another heavy sigh, he said, "We need to make our way to the barn. The Mighty Hooved One is waiting for us."

Marcel began barking orders at Stan and Louie to gather our things and prepare to make way.

Marcel looked nervously at them; they were crouched on the ground, huddled close together. They jumped to their feet, stumbling and running into each other, collecting the trays and chattering Georgia's name.

Geordie, still standing between Sager and me, curiously asked, "If no one other than Andre has seen Georgia and the only thing she said the day she took Martin was 'I've got you,' how do you know that Georgia is her name?"

Marcel replied quickly, "The myths have always referred to her as Georgia. Until now, I always thought she was just a scary bedtime story the elders told the children."

Geordie watched as Stan nervously listened and tugged at the last jug of carrot cider, awaiting our departure.

Geordie's eyes widened in suspense as he moved closer to gaze upon both Stan and Louie's faces. He said in a low menacing voice, "I, too, have heard the voice that haunts in the night."

Geordie cupped his tiny paws around his mouth, tilting his head to the sky, and said, "Who...? Who Do I Feed? Who...?"

Geordie squinted into the darkness over Stan and Louie's heads as if he saw Georgia. Imitating the sounds again, right into their faces, he barely whispered, "Who...? Who Do I Feed...? Who...?"

Turning away from Stan and Louie, he extended his arms; by the light of the fire, he cast a shadow on the ground as if to indicate wings. Swaying from side to side, he quietly said, "Her wings span over many other worlds. I've seen the large talons spread like claws as she swoops to the ground to grab her prey."

Suddenly, Geordie spun around, making a fast grasping motion with his paws at Stan and Louie. They were now entirely beside themselves with fear.

Stan jerked Louie to his feet and dragged him, stumbling into the tall grass. They huddled together in a tight ball, praying for the gods to protect them.

Geordie jumped into the tall grass, continuing to scare them, he said. "Once Georgia has you, you will never be seen again! Who...! Who...!" Geordie called out again with his paws curled into claws above his head.

Just then, Stan jumped to his feet and ran to the creek, leaving Louie behind. We could hear him still praying as he crossed through the water, disappearing into the night.

Geordie laughed as he picked up the half-empty jug of carrot cider Stan had left behind on the ground next to Louie. "That was easy enough." He laughed, removing the cork to have a sip.

I felt sorry for Stan, who was now on his way back to The Great Stone Ruins, and for Louie, who now sat alone, looking terrified.

"Do you know the punishments for abandoning a mission?" Marcel snapped at Louie. He nodded yes and jumped up to quickly finish gathering the trays.

We all watched while trying to hold our laughter at Geordie with his theatrics while taunting Stan and Louie. It was clear he only wanted the carrot cider and had never ever seen Georgia.

Marcel pulled the map from his pocket; carefully, he unfolded it. Andre then pointed on the map, telling Marcel how to approach the silo where the oats would be. They devised a plan, and we were finally on our way.

We all struggled through the wet grass. As Andre had indicated earlier, the cattails were thick and provided a much-needed cover. The grass was covered in pollen that had fallen from the tops of the cattails.

Sager began to sneeze uncontrollably. Her eyes were watering, and she stopped to clean the sticky pollen from her face.

Andre signaled from the front that we needed to be quiet and wait. I sat up to get a better view. We had finally made it to the barn.

A strange little four-legged animal was inside the fence, not much bigger than my sister and me. He had long, sharp horns that curled over his back. Around his neck hung a brass bell. He made a strange neighing sound.

Could this be The Mighty Hooved One, I thought? Andre was already on the other side of the fence, and we watched as he skirted the perimeter, disappearing into the barn.

Geordie stumbled around as he ripped a cattail from the ground. The murky water dripped from the roots down his front. From the way he giggled, we could tell that he had finished Stan's jug of carrot cider.

Geordie lovingly smelled the entire length of the cattail. He removed the pollen that clung to the top of the cattail, looking at it adoringly while saying, "If only my sweet Betty were here." Then he popped the sticky pollen into his mouth and closed his eyes. We watched as he made a motion with his paw, like the one my Mommy calls a 'chef's kiss.' Then wistfully, he said, "Betty could make the best cattail soup known throughout my lands."

Geordie licked his fingers and pulled more sticky pollen from the top of the cattail. He offered Sager and me a bite, saying, "I wish I had me some butter!" Then he leaned against the fence to relax and enjoy his feast.

I noticed the strange little horned animal had climbed to the top of his food bin. Looking in our direction, he spied us. He jumped into the air and began rushing toward the fence. Marcel called for us to move back.

Geordie, still licking the pollen from his fingers and wishing for seconds, had not heard the call for a retreat. From the safety of the cattails, Sager and I tried to warn him.

The funny little animal ran at Geordie with his head down. Sager and I were still whispering for Geordie to take cover.

Geordie stood up when the horned animal butted him from behind. The strange little animal neighed, saying, "Bullseye!" As he sent Geordie flying through the air back into the cattails.

We heard Geordie land in the murky water calling out for his Betty yet again. Sputtering, he came out of the water, ready for a fight. His tiny paws balled into fists, swinging madly as he pushed his way back through the cattails saying, "Where, uh I mean, who did that? Nobody sneaks up on Geordie Jakensen! Show yourself!"

Marcel tried to pull Geordie back into the cattails, but it was too late. The strange animal had already seen us, and he raced towards the fence again. Thankfully his aim was not so successful this time.

Marcel asked who was carrying the bota bag and then said we would need it to fill our bags with the oats. Sager and I said at the same time, "Geordie has it."

Geordie turned and grunted, "Geordie has what?" Referring to himself in the third person. Because he was agitated at being hit and thrown into the cattails.

"The bota bag," I said, "where is it? Marcel needs it so we can get going."

Reaching to his neck, Geordie searched. Worried, he said, "It was right here. I must have lost it when I flew into the cattails." He shook his tiny fist at the fence again. Marcel ordered Louie to take Geordie to immediately look for the bota bag in the cattails.

"We cannot retrieve the oats if we don't have the carrot cider. Andre will be trapped in the barn with The Mighty Hooved One; we must hurry!" Marcel exclaimed.

Reluctantly, Geordie followed Louie to look for the bag, still cursing and rubbing at his backside.

Marcel went over the plan while we waited. He told us that we needed the strange little animal to go to sleep. He said, "The carrot cider needs to go into the trough, and it will take a few minutes to work its magic."

Then Marcel emphasized. "One of you will have to dump the cider unnoticed into his trough. It will take a skilled and fast movement to avoid his horns."

I felt the excitement rising in my chest. I hoped it would be me. At home, I was the fastest in the yard every day. My brother, Mr. Wienie, always sounded the charges, but I always led the way. I felt confident I would be chosen.

Sager sniffed the air, trying to familiarize herself with her surroundings; as the horned animal continued ramming the fence, she asked Marcel, "What kind of animal is this?"

Marcel explained that Billy was an old goat. "He was brought here to look after Flash, who we know and lovingly call The Mighty Hooved One. Flash is old and blind now. He used to be a racehorse, and old Billy once told us he was like a flash of lighting as the thunder rolled from his hooves. That's how The Mighty Hooved One got his name."

Sager's ears perked up. She said, "That's the thunder! That's what we are hearing!" She exclaimed, "I knew that sound didn't come from the sky."

Marcel continued telling us the plan. "Andre will open the doors. You two will leave a trail of apples to the silo. It will take twenty-four apples spaced evenly across the ground. You each have twelve in your packs. Flash will know and return to the barn if you miss even one apple. Once you have them in place, I will knock on the door, Andre will let Flash out. He will eat the trail of apples leading him to the silo. Once he stops, one of you will have to jump to his back and then jump onto the silo. You must travel the stairs to the bottom of the silo quickly. Grab the red handle on the wall and pull it down. The oats will fall from that pipe hanging over Billy's trough." Marcel said while pointing at each location we needed to be to accomplish this.

Geordie was celebrating loudly, crawling back through the cattails holding the bota bag above his head. The old goat pawed at the ground, ramming the fence with his head again. We all jumped back.

Sager bared her teeth and asked, "What's this old goat's name again, and what is his problem?!"

"Sager, his name is Billy, and I want to be the one who pours the cider in his trough." I said excitedly.

Geordie quickly replied, "I wouldn't want to go anywhere near those horns!"

Sager stepped in front of me and said, "No, Elizabeth, Billy is too mean; you could be hurt, let Louie do it."

Louie was trying to lick the sticky pollen from his feet. He looked like he was wearing fluffy white slippers. He said, "I can barely move without sticking to the ground." Then he asked, "How can I run?"

We could hear Flash's hooves as they stomped the ground because he could smell the odor of the skunks causing him to be anxious. Marcel said, "You all need to decide who is going to dump the bota bag. I am the only one big enough to open the door from the outside. It will have to be one of you four who puts the carrot cider in the trough."

"Sager, please let me do it; all we have done through this whole smelly journey is follow these guys. I need to show them that I can do this." I pleaded with Sager, "Please, sister! Please let me do it."

Sager sat down to think, snapping her attention at Geordie. She said, "Okay, sister, you can go, but only if Geordie goes with you."

Geordie backed away, holding his backside, saying, "I'm in no big hurry to play with that Billy goat and his sharp horns again!"

While protesting, he held the bota bag in the air, trying to give it away to anyone that would take it.

Through the sticky pollen that was now all over his face, Louie said, "You have enjoyed the carrot cider throughout this journey, haven't you, Geordie? What's left in the bota bag is the last little bit. Once Billy is asleep, you can finish what he doesn't drink. What do you think about that?"

Now inspired to have a taste, Geordie rubbed at his belly and jumped to my back.

Flash was kicking at the sides of the barn now. Through the window in his stall, we could see him rising up and down, thrusting his front legs wildly in the air.

Marcel taunted Billy in the opposite direction, leading the old goat away from us. Keeping Billy's attention while daring him to ram the fence.

Marcel hollered loudly over his shoulder and said, "Follow the fence until you see the trough, cut through the barnyard, and dump the cider. Then we will wait for Billy to fall asleep."

I climbed through the fence with Geordie on my back. I could feel the dirt flying from my paws as I ran with all my might. It was marvelous. I felt free. The danger of Billy seeing us added to my excitement.

Geordie had leaned forward while grasping my ears, we rounded the barnyard. He was tugging down on my right ear when he said, pointing, "There it is! There's the trough; you missed it. Turn around."

Billy saw us as I looped back towards the trough. Leaving Marcel standing at the fence, he charged at us; and in a satisfied voice, the old Billy goat announced, "Here comes the Ole Bullseye!"

Geordie screamed and said, "Oh my sweet Betty! He wants more of Geordie Jakensen." He yelled, pulling wildly at my ears in all directions, and frantically screamed, "Run faster, Elizabeth! Jump! Jump right now!"

Jump? I thought. "What am I supposed to jump over?" I asked him. He didn't answer. He was jerking my ears up and down, kicking his heels into my sides, trying to get me to run faster or jump.

Geordie was in a frenzy. The sound of the bell that hung from Billy's neck was getting louder.

"Here he comes!" Geordie screamed as he pulled back on my ears. His grip was tight with fear. We were in front of Billy's food bin, and I had come to a fast halt. Geordie flew over my head and landed in the empty trough.

Billy ran between us, missing Geordie. He hit the side of the silo with full force. Stumbling to his feet, he spun around, trying to focus his eyes.

"Quick, Geordie, dump the cider!" I yelled.

Geordie jumped to his feet, jerked the bota bag from his neck, bit through the bota bag, offered it to the sky, saying, "Here's to you and me, Betty." He crossed himself, took a quick sip, then dumped the remaining cider into the trough.

Billy started pawing the ground, looking first at me, then at Geordie. "Hurry, Geordie," I heard Sager yell from the fence, "you can make it back to Elizabeth."

Geordie's tiny paws clawed at the sides of the trough. He kept sliding back into the cider. Each time allowing him to get another big drink. It was just too slick. Finally, Geordie made it to the top and stood on the edge. Seeing this, the old goat stepped back.

Billy lined himself up with Geordie. He lowered his head and ran full force landing his horns on Geordie's backside once more.

Fortunately, he had slid one too many times back into the cider. And he flew through the air, laughing maniacally.

"For the love of Betty's hot buttered biscuits, here I come!" Geordie shouted as I jumped to catch him mid-air.

After laughing to himself, Billy stopped to have a long drink from his trough. Lifting his head, he neighed, saying, "What's this?" Smacking his lips, he continued to drink.

I placed Geordie on the ground beside Louie, whose swollen tongue hung out the side of his mouth from repeatedly licking at the sticky pollen which entirely covered his body.

I laughed because he looked like Dinkelman, Mr. Wienie's fuzzy teddy bear.

"This pollen is everywhere; it's not coming off." Louie complained.

Sager sniffed at the air and told him, "It's an improvement as far as I'm concerned." And then she laughed.

We gathered our backpacks, climbed back through the fence, and waited for Billy to fall asleep. Flash had calmed down. I looked up into the tree, wondering again about Georgia. Something moved up there, so I rubbed at my eyes. I thought I caught a glimpse of long claw-like talons.

Blinking, I looked again. Did I really see that? Maybe, I thought it was only the nighttime sky playing tricks on me.

Billy started singing to himself in a slurred, sleepy voice. His song referred to someone named Henry the Eighth.

Hiccupping, he sang, *"I'm 'Henry the Eighth, I am,' Henery the Eighth I am I am! I got married to the widow next door…She's been married seven times before… Second verse! Same as the First!"*

Billy sat down on his haunches and slumped over, still mumbling the song.

Sager and I crept a little closer. We were almost past him when the pollen floating in the air caused Sager to sneeze several times, and Billy sat up. "Oh, no!" I said out loud. Sager and Billy were face to face right now.

"Do not move; he will fall back asleep if you are patient." Marcel whispered loudly from the door of the barn.

Billy belched in Sager's face while saying, "I'm Henry the Eighth!"

Then old goat said while laughing, "No! I'm Carson, Carson T. Justice to be exact." Banging his horns against the trough, he slurred, "This is the justice I deliver."

Billy belched again and continued with his name. "The T! Well, that's just extra. I like it." He slurred and mumbled, enunciating each word of Carson T. Justice, with a bang of his horns against the side of his trough. Billy giggled a little and finished up by saying, "Besides, I think it sounds fancy."

Sager fanned the air with her paw. She could smell the fermented cider lofting from his breath. Billy fell back asleep for a second.

Belching again, he opened one eye, pulling Sager closer to his face as he laughed and said, "The T isn't fancy. It's for T Time!"

T Time? I thought. Maybe he meant teatime?

I whispered to Sager, "Is he talking about the kind of tea like grandma drinks?"

"I'm not sure, Elizabeth." Sager said, trying to pull away from Billy.

Struggling to his feet, Billy's horns clacked against the trough as he took another long drink. He swung his front paw in the air, causing him to fall down again. Lifting his head, he hiccupped and neighed the word "FOUR," then he laughed again, saying, "they never see the Ole Bullseye while they're swinging their golf clubs do they?" He was still giggling, recalling how they make such easy targets.

Sager started to hum the little song Billy had been singing. She gently repeated what he had sung. "*Second verse! Same as the First.*"

Billy went back to sleep, singing the first verse. Sager and I made our way over to the barn. We started laying out the trail with the apples. Sager went first, counting her way to twelve. We were halfway across the barnyard. I opened my bag and picked up where she had left off. I placed eight apples all the way to the trough. Four more, and we would be all the way to the silo.

"That's it, Bethy, Nine, Ten, Eleven," Sager said while counting the last few out loud. I could tell she was excited.

We were finally going to fill our bags and return home. It had been a long stinky journey. Even though I craved adventure every day, I was ready for a nap in my own bed, and I missed home and Mommy.

As I reached for the last apple, I discovered the pack was empty. Panicking, I said, as I searched through the bag, "Oh no, one is missing, Sager, it's missing! What are we going to do?"

The Queen's words rang loudly in my head, 'lest The Mighty Hooved One should know!'

Marcel also said that Flash would return to the barn if there was a break in the trail of apples. I frantically repeated over and over, "What are we going to do?"

Sager took the pack and looked inside. I could tell she was becoming frustrated. She looked up at the silo. "We can still do it, Elizabeth." She said, "It will be a long jump. You'll have to do it. I don't think I can because my legs are shorter than yours. Do you think you can do it?" She asked with concern in her voice. Shaking me with her paw, she asked again, "Elizabeth, did you hear me? Do you think you can do it?"

I looked at the silo, following the pipe with my eyes. I measured how far I would have to jump. "It would be a long jump." I said aloud.

I worried that we wouldn't have any more apples to lead Flash if I misjudged the distance.

Nodding her head yes, Sager asked me again, "Do you think you can do it?"

I froze and then leaned into Sager. She licked the dirt and sweat from my face. Reminding me again of who I was, Sager said, "You are Sargent of Airs, Elizabeth! Nothing can stop you or hold you down."

Sager called me by my yard name. Our brother, Mr. Wienie, had assigned us individual names to be used while playing outside in our yard at home.

I am Sargent of Airs because of my ability to jump and fly through the air. We weren't just playing in the yard this time, and I was afraid. It wasn't a game directed at getting treats, it was for real, this time, and I felt scared.

CHAPTER 12

WITH THE APPLES IN PLACE, SAGER AND I WATCHED FROM the top of Billy's food bin as Marcel knocked on the door, signaling Andre to open it.

The door creaked, and my heart thumped loudly; the time had come, and Sager was so confident I could make the jump.

I could hear Flash's hooves as he left the barn. His enormous nostrils sniffed the ground, searching for the first apple. Finding it, he mouthed the apple. Then he followed the trail slowly.

He stopped short of the last apple, and my heart raced. I wondered whether I had placed the last apple too far apart.

Quickly, Andre ran to kick the apple in Flash's direction. At the same time, Billy let out a loud snort and rolled over, causing Flash to raise his head; Flash missed the scent of the apple as it rolled by.

Flash returned his nose to the ground. His tail swished as small clouds of dust formed around his nose; he searched for the scent of the next apple and couldn't find it. I panicked as Flash slowly turned and headed back to the barn.

Andre called out. "Hurry! We need to hold him there! If Flash can't find that apple, he'll return to the barn."

Marcel and Andre scurried around the old blind racehorse, stopping just short of the barn entrance. They feverishly waved their tails in the air, emitting little clouds of stench. While moving backward, they returned Flash to the center of the barnyard.

Flash's nostrils flared from the foul odor. He was becoming enraged, jerking his head in every direction as he stomped the ground. Andre hollered to Marcel, "Circle back and flank him to the right; I'll hold him here."

Andre's tail fluttered in the air as he continued to emit the foul odor. Marcel dodged through Flashes hooves, trying to nip at his heels. Marcel missed. Flash was out of control. Lunging forward, trying to stomp Andre.

Marcel attempted to nip at his back heels again. Flash kicked his back legs, sending Marcel flying through the air, slamming him into the fence. Sager and I both raced to his side.

Marcel opened his eyes, looked at Sager, and said, "You must nip at the heels. It's the only way to get him to run." Then he coughed.

Suddenly terrified, Sager backed away; moving her head side to side, she said, "I was sent away for biting. I was locked in a cage for six months until my Mommy rescued me. I don't do that anymore! I love my family and my home! I don't want to be sent away again."

Andre said in a loud voice as he was struggled to hold his ground. "We need to flank Flash to the right. He must run in a circle."

The stench that hung in the air made my eyes burn. I could see Andre dodging the old blind horse's giant hooves as he closed the door to the barn. Unable to get into the barn, Flash paced back and forth now. Raising his head, calling to the sky.

Putting my paw on Sager's foot, I told her this one time it would be okay, and I knew Mommy would agree it would be okay to nip at the old horse's heels.

Then that special twinkle flashed in her eye, and she agreed to do it. Sager called out to me as she ran toward Flash, "Get into position, Elizabeth. I will run him past you."

Flash had calmed down by the time I returned to Billy's food bin. He was still standing in front of the barn door. A gentle breeze had lifted the foul odor from the barnyard. I watched as Sager began to bite at the old horse's front heels.

He only lifted his leg and swatted at the air with his tail. Sager hadn't nipped hard enough. She moved in again, biting harder at the other front heel. Flash raised his head. Now he was well aware something had happened.

I could hear Sager apologizing before she sunk her teeth in again. Andre stood winded nearby; he called out, "Go for the right foot, now the left."

Sager did as Andre instructed, and Flash backed away from the barn door in a hurry. Sager nipped him again and again, making him throw his head to the sky once more; Flash turned, running to the center of the barnyard, away from her.

Flash began to run in a circle. The ground shook as he ran faster. A cloud of dust was forming again. By the way Sager was barking, I could tell she was enjoying herself as she chased him.

The old racehorse rounded the barnyard as they approached me. Sager called out, "Jump, Bethy! Jump now he's right in front of you."

I panicked and froze as Flash swiftly passed by. Sager saw I hadn't jumped. She quickened her pace, barking louder and biting as she herded Flash through the barnyard once more.

The old racehorses' hooves pounded the ground, and he was breathing hard; they rounded the fence again.

Leaping into the air, I landed on Flash's back, and within a few paces, he stopped and began kicking his back legs high into the air.

Andre and Sager backed away from the massive cloud of dust that was forming again. Flash's powerful hooves pounded the ground over and over.

It was time for me to make the long jump. I turned toward the silo, then counted one two three.

I couldn't jump. I was terrified; what if I missed. All the while, visions of home and my family ran through my head.

My legs trembled as I struggled to stay on the old horse. I had to do this. Flash threw his back legs into the air once more; this was it. I thought to myself, it was now or never.

I jumped forward with all my might. As I flew through the air, I could see the ground below me. The side of the silo was in front of me now, and I was falling. Suddenly, something caught me, and I felt myself being hoisted higher into the sky. I heard a kind voice say, "I've got you, Mommy's Little Bit." And I was gently set on top of the silo.

I turned to see who had spoken to me. Nothing was there. Had I imagined this, had I really made the long jump? I was sure I felt something catch me in the air.

The dust settled, Geordie and Louie now stood with the others. Marcel had recovered. Geordie sobered up, and I was relieved to see them.

I could hear Sager as she chanted my name. Flash had returned to his stall in the barn. Billy lay restless, pawing at the air. Letting out an occasional nay.

Andre called out, "Go through that small door and down the steps till you find a red handle on the wall; pull down on it."

I opened the door to darkness; the smell of molasses and warm oats filled my nose. The stairs that Andre mentioned were in front of me. Leaning against the handrail, I descended the stairs; they were steep and long. I carefully felt for each step that spiraled along the inside wall, thinking about the soft, comforting voice I had heard. I stopped and wondered again whether I really made the long jump.

"No, I was falling." I said aloud to myself. Then I thought, how did I land on the top of the silo.

My mind raced, trying to recall what had happened. Not realizing I was standing in front of the red handle, I stood talking aloud to myself.

I remembered! I heard the voice say, 'I've got you, Mommy's Little Bit.' "But who in this world besides Sager would know that is my nickname?" I said aloud.

"Georgia, was it you?" I said loud enough, causing my words to echo throughout the silo. I was talking to myself, forgetting what I was supposed to be doing. "Could that have been you, Georgia?" I spoke.

Sager was scratching at the door and calling for me. Yelling, she said, "Open this door, Bethy! Who are you talking to? Elizabeth James, are you okay!? Can you hear me?" Quickly I pulled on the red handle, and I could hear the oats sifting to the ground.

Sager was still clawing at the door barking now with excitement, "Bethy, you're a hero! You did it! Come out so we can go home." She said, celebrating.

Pushing on the door in front of me, it swung open with a huge bang. Billy snorted and sat up. Everyone froze. Andre held his paw to his lips and whispered, "Shush, maybe he will go back to sleep."

Struggling to his feet, Billy looked around. "What's going on here?" He neighed. He was still feeling the effects of the fermented cider. His legs wobbled, and he sat back down. "What a dream! A red dog flying through the air." He said, then shook his head.

Billy loudly belched, then he said, "Caught by a…," then the old goat faded back to sleep.

Geordie stood with his backside to Sager breathing a sigh of relief as Billy went back to sleep. Dancing around, moving his feet swiftly, and dodging from side to side, saying, "I'm ready this time." Waving his tiny fists into the air. He said, "Lucky for that old goat that he went back to sleep."

Andre went back into the silo, pulled the handle, and closed the door. He then called for Marcel and Louie to fill the backpacks with oats.

Seeing the new feast that now lay on the ground, Geordie dove in to have a bite. Even though Louie was covered in the sticky pollen, he jumped in right behind Geordie. Seeing the pair enjoying the oats, Marcel and Andre also joined in.

Geordie emerged from the oats with his cheeks full and asked, "What did that old goat say?"

Marcel swallowed what was in his mouth and replied, "Billy must have seen Elizabeth as she jumped from Flash's back." He pointed to the top of the silo, showing it was a long jump.

Louie said, "I didn't think she would make it, but she did."

The molasses mixed with oats stuck to the pollen that covered Louie's body.

We could only see his eyes. He no longer resembled a skunk, let alone any other animal. Sager and I rested as the Geordie and skunks finished satisfying their hunger.

Billy fell back to sleep without finishing his statement. It sounded like he saw what had caught me in the air. The others did not realize what he was trying to say.

I knew I didn't make the long jump by myself. Something had helped me to the top of the silo. "Was it Georgia's voice I heard as she caught me?" I said out loud.

I looked at Andre, remembering his story of Martin. He told us that Georgia said, 'I've got you.' Then she flew away with Martin. I wondered why she had set me on top of the silo instead of flying away with me.

Georgia had helped me, and I felt confused. "Maybe she helped those around her and was just misunderstood." I whispered aloud.

Sager said with her head cocked to the side. "Who's misunderstood? Don't worry about me, Elizabeth. I will never bite again." I was talking out loud to myself again. Sager was listening and thought I was talking about her.

When Mommy brought my sister home, she was told, 'This puppy has a biting problem. That's why she had been adopted so many times.'

To which Mommy replied, 'I don't care. This baby is misunderstood. I am taking her home anyway.'

Sager was misunderstood and wasn't happy until she saw our Mommy in her new home.

I lay there looking up into the tree. Geordie and the skunks were now sleeping. Sager was stretched out on her side. My eyes felt heavy; I scanned the sky looking for Georgia, thinking of Mommy and hoping we would be home soon.

CHAPTER 13

I OPENED MY EYES TO SEE MULTI-COLORED FURRY MASKED animals running their paws over Sager's collar. One of them was tugging at her charms.

Sager was enjoying the way they nibbled at her ears, and she said, "Not yet, Mommy, I'm still sleepy."

I rubbed my eyes, unsure if I was dreaming. Slowly I sat up, seeing that these animals were everywhere.

Sager stretched and said, "Not now, Bethy, lay back down, then we'll go out in a little while."

Geordie sprang to his feet, causing Marcel and Andre to sit up. They reached for their swords, but they were nowhere to be found. The masked animals were still piled on Sager; she kicked with her hind feet half asleep.

The masked animals took her collar off. They passed it around, smelling it. One of them put her collar on, and I started barking, saying, "Give that back! It's not yours."

Geordie wiped at the drool hanging from his mouth and said, "So you're trying to steal from Geordie Jakensen?"

Sager finally sat up, looked around, springing to her feet; she was unaware they had taken her collar. "What's going on? Elizabeth, are you okay? They didn't bite you, did they?" Sager asked, inching her way towards me.

Andre stepped carefully backward with his paws in the air, saying, "Easy, don't make any sudden movements. Where is Louie?" Then he whispered to Marcel, "Do you have your sword?"

Marcel shook his head no, "They took my sword while we were sleeping. There are too many of them." He said, sounding worried.

The masked animals were still circling us, hissing and laughing as they rubbed their front paws together.

I glanced where Louie was sleeping. The molasses and oats had matted in his fur, and he could not move. He was stuck to the ground; all he could move was his eyes.

We all stood with our backs to each other as they continued to circle. Sager bared her teeth and said, "They are wearing my collar! They've got our backpacks and your weapons too." Pointing to Marcel and Andre's swords.

Geordie jumped to my back and whispered in my ear, "I've seen this gaze of outlaws before. They will rob you blind!"

"What is a gaze of outlaws?" I asked, feeling scared.

Andre answered, "Gaze is how these Outlaws are referred to as a group. They're raccoons, sneaky, thieving raccoons." He said, snatching his sword from the one in front of him.

Marcel quickly reached for his sword as well. He was too slow, and the raccoon sneered and moved in closer.

The masked animals stomped their feet and began chanting, "Robby, Robby...." They chanted over and over.

The chanting crowd began to step aside, and what appeared to be their leader approached us. He walked with a limp and had an eye patch. He was missing spots of fur. A spoon was tied around his neck.

Geordie called out, pointing over my head at the leader and grasping at my neck. He said, "Look, he's wearing Stan's apron and helmet!" Covering his mouth, he trembled with fear.

The tattered raccoon stopped and looked at Geordie; with a creepy snicker, he said, "Stan? Was that his name?"

All the Outlaws laughed as they reached forward to congratulate their leader. He raised his paws to silence his gang. He snapped his fingers, and a small table and chair were placed before him. He sat down and propped his feet on Louie, who was still stuck to the ground and resembled a huge rock.

The band of Outlaws had not yet discovered Louie, and his eyes were now screaming out in fear.

The tattered raccoon sat down on the chair, leaned forward with his elbows on the table, and asked, "What do we have here?" Then he laughed.

He snapped his fingers again and held out his hand, demanding something from his gang.

One of the Outlaws burst forward, removing a goblet from the bag hanging around his waist, and placed it in his leader's hand. Another one of the Outlaws quickly filled the goblet with what appeared to be cider.

The tattered raccoon took a long sip, wiped his mouth with the back of his paw, and said, "I am Robby, and these are my Band of Bandits!" Gesturing to the other raccoons that were holding our things.

"What kind of treasures have we found here?" Robby asked with a mischievous tone in his voice.

The Bandit that had Sager's collar on stepped to the table, removed it, and placed it before Robby. The other Bandits put the rest of our things at his feet. Robby sifted through the packs, spilling the oats to the ground.

He picked up Marcel's sword and yielded it to the sky. "This should work just fine." He laughed and said, "Yes, very nice indeed." Then he tossed the sword to one of the Bandits standing nearby.

Marcel took a step closer, the Bandit holding the sword pointed it at him. Robby said, waving his finger from side to side, "No, no, no! Be still like a good little warrior. This will only take a minute! Then we will be on our way!"

Robby's voice was deep and raspy as he continued to say, "Here, see how this suits you."

He tossed Marcel and Andre's shields into the crowd of Bandits as if he were being generous; I could tell he enjoyed being a bully.

Robby snapped his fingers again, and his goblet was filled once more. He looked us over while he adjusted his feet on Louie's back.

Poor Louie was still stuck to the ground, and his eyes widened as he looked at us, pleading for help.

Robby drummed his fingers on the table, then stood up and grabbed Sager's collar. Spinning it around his finger, the charms made a soft clinking sound. He was looking at Andre and laughing as he approached us.

Andre stood with his back to Marcel. Andre's sword was at his side, ready to strike forward. Robby stopped in front of Marcel and asked, "Do you like my helmet? Look, I'm one of you now; I'm a Warrior Skunk." Robby said as he pretended to march.

Then Robby leaned in over the top of Geordie and me; he whispered in a loud voice, "What was his name again?"

Robby was referring to Stan's helmet while browbeating Geordie. I felt fearful, knowing that these terrible Bandits probably bullied Stan into giving them his things.

Geordie trembled with fear, hiding his face in my neck. Robby's breath was hot as he laughed in my face.

Andre grasped at his sword. Marcel reached to restrain Andre and said, "He is only brave because of his Band of Bandits. Let him have his fun, so he will leave."

Robby looked into Marcel's eyes and said, "So you're the new one the old skunk Queen sent to watch after dear ole Andre."

Robby patted Andre on the face and then whispered into his ear, "Still letting your anger get the best of you?" He asked and then laughed.

Andre grabbed at Robby while saying, "You won't get away this time." The Bandits hissed and moved in closer.

Laughing, Robby held up his hand to stop the Bandits and said, "The Queen's personal guards have never caught me!"

Robby pushed Andre to the ground, then jumped to the top of the tiny table again, put his paws on his hips, and proclaimed, "Many have tried, all of them have failed!" Then he raised both arms into the air and asked the Bandits, "For who am I?"

Jumping up and down, his Band of Bandits chanted his name again. While Robby stood on the table, I could see scars from an old injury. His left hind leg was mangled.

Robby stopped to look at the charms on Sager's collar. Reading the name aloud, he raised his paw to silence his gang and asked us, "Which one of you is Mommy's Babysitter?"

I sucked in my breath; I was afraid Sager would try to fight him. Robby almost sang the words. I couldn't take my eyes off him.

I stood there with the others feeling helpless; I thought to myself, what were we going to do.

I saw Marcel glance down at Louie. I watched as Louie moved his front paw ever so slightly. Marcel shook his head no, indicating for Louie to remain still.

Robby jumped back to the ground and finished his drink. Holding Sager's collar in front of him, his voice became more forceful as he looked at his Bandits and asked again, "Who did you take this off of?"

Sager cleared her throat and declared, "I am Mommy's Babysitter, and you, sir, are nothing more than a cowardly con artist and a bully! Now give me back my collar; my Mommy bought that for me."

Just then, Sager looked at me and winked with that bit of a twinkle in her eye. She was up to something. Sager taunted Robby back, telling him it was a unique collar. Then she yelled, "My Mommy bought that, especially for me!"

Geordie raised his head and snickered, laughing as he said, "You're gonna get it now!"

Robby snapped his head back in Geordie's direction and laughed. It sounded evil as he lowered his voice and rubbed his paws together. "Who does Mommy's Babysitter think she is?" He asked as he turned towards his Bandits.

Robby stalked in and out of his gang, whispering to them, "Are you really going to allow a groundhog to speak to your leader this way?" Still circling his Bandits, he added, "Who takes care of you?"

The Bandits all whispered back, "You do, boss."

Robby raised his voice to a shrill as he moved back to the table and said, "Who took you in when every door was slammed in your face? Who feeds you on long cold nights?" He worked the Bandits into a frenzy, and they began to pound the ground with their feet chanting, Robby! Over and over.

Robby held Sager's collar into the air and started to mock her; he said, "Look at me, I'm Mommy's Babysitter!" He put Sager's collar on and asked the cheering Bandits, "Do you like what My Mommy bought for me?"

I couldn't take it anymore; I started to bark. I had never felt anger like this before. I was tired of feeling afraid. I looked from Sager to Andre. I thought, how would we make him stop and leave us alone.

Robby turned and kicked our backpacks, sending them rolling across the ground.

Sager started to growl while kicking her hind legs one at a time; Marcel put his hand on Sager's back and said yet again, "Let them have their fun so they will leave."

Robby asked Sager with a snicker, "What's so special about this collar?" The Bandits were all laughing and whistling.

Robby was trying to really embarrass my sister now as he pranced around, waving her collar directly in her face.

Sager sat down and began to laugh. Robby stopped and asked the Bandits, "Who says she can laugh?"

Sager told him, "Snap the last buckle, see how it fits you. You might like it! I promise you this, you will give me back my charms!"

Robby bent over and slapped his knee, laughing as he said, "I really like this one." He laughed harder, winked, and pointed at Sager, asking, "Would you like to be one of my Bandits?" Raising the collar above his head, Robby skipped towards his Bandits, singing, "I'm Mommy's Babysitter." Over and over.

Sager was trying to hold her laughter as Robby skipped around. She told Geordie, "When I say, go, run and grab my charms. Mr. Bully can keep that miserable old collar."

We all looked at Sager with curiosity. Smiling, she paused and then told us to keep watching Robby.

Reaching for the last buckle, Robby secured the collar around his neck, turned, and bowed to his Bandits.

Marcel and Andre looked at Sager. Geordie asked, "What are you talking about?"

Sager explained that it was her barking collar that Robby had on. She said, "It only works if both buckles are snapped. It will tighten around his neck when he talks, but if he yells or screams, it will shock him."

Robby spun on his heel and bowed in our direction. He was going to mock Sager once more but only stopped and tugged at the collar.

Robby's eyes bulged as he cleared his throat. He thrashed around, throwing his head from side to side, running in circles letting out short little screams. Puzzled at what was happening, the Bandits stepped closer to help Robby.

Sager whispered to us all, "Get ready to grab our things." Then she began to laugh. "How does your boss look in my collar now?" She asked the Bandits.

Robby bent over, backing up, grasping at the buckles. The Bandits rushed forward to help him. We all began to laugh when suddenly Louie had freed himself, and he sprung up from the ground.

Louie's eyes were huge. One arm was stuck to his chin, the other was attached to his forehead. He was grunting as he struggled to free his arms.

The Bandits all froze in terror at the sight of Louie. The sticky pollen mixed with oats and molasses was dripping from his face. He was dirty. His fur was matted with straw, adding to his size. A tumbleweed was stuck on top of his head, giving him the appearance of one scary antler.

Robby had not seen Louie as they collided, and both fell to the ground. Robby landed face first with Louie on his back. Sager yelled, "Now, Geordie, grab my charms!"

Geordie leaped from my back and dove between Robby and Louie. Geordie started jerking at the charms. Geordie, Louie, and Robby screamed simultaneously as all three were being shocked by Sager's collar.

Geordie was now trapped between Robby and Louie while they thrashed around on the ground. He pulled too hard at the charms, causing the second buckle to be released; Robby stood up, leaving Louie lying on his back. Geordie was stuck to Louie's neck. Robby took the collar off and tried to hand it to one of the Bandits.

The Bandits had backed away. They were still in shock at the sight of Louie. Rubbing his throat, Robby sniffed Louie on the ground; it was the first time he didn't have something witty to say.

Geordie wiggled his tiny feet in the air, trying to free himself from the sticky mess in Louie's fur. Robby glanced at Sager and said, "I've changed my mind about you."

Robby grabbed Geordie from Louie's neck, looked into his eyes, and asked the Bandits if they thought he would make a nice treat for the birds. I felt afraid, and I couldn't breathe. We needed to do something to help Geordie.

Robby snapped his fingers, but the Bandits did not move. He looked in their direction and held his arms out. The Bandits had not responded to their boss's wants.

Robby stepped forward and grabbed the goblet he had been drinking from. He threw the liquid from his goblet in Louie's face. Frustrated, he said, "This monster is nothing more than a skunk covered in oats and molasses."

The sticky mess washed away, and we could see Louie's face once more. All the Bandits hissed and chattered to each other.

Then Robby tossed Geordie to the Bandits, and they shoved him in one of our backpacks.

Robby turned back towards us, looked around, and asked, "Where did dear old Andre go?" Sager turned and looked for him as well; I was not aware that Andre had left.

Louie managed to get to his feet and tried to answer Robby's question. Marcel quickly corrected Louie and motioned for him to stand with us.

I was terrified and wanted to go home. I could still see Geordie struggling to free himself from the backpack.

Robby called out to his Bandits, "What happens when someone leaves without permission?"

The Bandits' chatter became louder as they circled us. I couldn't take it any longer. I started barking, baring my teeth at the Bandits. I tried with all my might to scare them. They continued to move in closer.

Robby laughed, threw his head back, crying with a mocking scared little voice, and said, "Look, the little puppy is trying to bully us!"

He laughed harder and stepped closer. Bending over with his paws on his knees, looking into my face, he asked me, "Who is going to stop me? I'm so afraid!" Robby laughed in my face again. I felt afraid and wondered where Andre had gone.

Suddenly, all the Bandits began to run. I could hear Billy's bell ringing. "A bigger bully, that's who's going to stop you!" Billy neighed as he rammed his head into Robby's backside. Robby flew through the air. Billy laughed and shouted, "Bullseye!"

Billy ran at the rest of the Bandits, sending them flying through the air. I ran to grab the backpack Geordie was in. Sager chased a few of the Bandits herself; she enjoyed biting at their heels. Marcel chased after Robby.

Billy worked himself up and was pawing the ground; all the Bandits were gone now. It was just us standing in the barnyard.

Louie's eyes were huge as he screamed out and covered his head, realizing Billy was aiming for him; he tried to run, but his hindfoot was stuck to the ground. Billy sent him flying through the air into the cattails and murky water.

With Geordie still in the backpack, Sager helped me through the fence. Louie came cleanly out of the small pond; he no longer looked like something from another world. He was holding his backside as he walked towards us, saying, "I don't know if I should be mad or thank old Billy."

We laughed as Geordie emerged from the backpack holding Sager's collar in his tiny paw. "Look what they forgot, *'bonnie lass!'* " He spoke. Lovingly smiling at Sager, placing the collar around Sager's neck, Geordie gently nuzzled her neck, and she licked his face.

As Marcel and Andre returned, Billy was still pawing the ground and ramming the fence with his horns. Andre was carrying Stan's helmet and apron.

I still felt sorry for Stan, and I now positively knew that Robby had also bullied him.

It was Billy who had saved us from Robby. Andre had snuck away to wake the cranky old goat, and it was Billy who rescued us from Robby and his Band of Bandits.

As we gathered our things and prepared to leave, I turned to look up into the tree one last time, wondering again about Georgia. Could it have been her voice that I heard? Was she the one that helped me to the top of the Silo?

CHAPTER 14

NDRE LED US BACK THROUGH THE CATTAILS. SWIFTLY WE made our way to the edge of the Second Kingdom, where we crossed again through the creek back into The Field of Mystery and Wonderment. Marcel and Louie made a small fire for us to warm ourselves by. Geordie told Marcel and Andre how Billy sent Louie flying through the air.

I asked Andre how he knew Robby and his Band of Bandits. Andre said. "I have chased Robby for years now. He always manages to escape. Robby is known very well throughout the Three Kingdoms. He likes to bully folks and forces them to become outlaws. If he is refused, he will bully them more, sometimes even worse."

We sat quietly for a few more hours and rested by the fire. I wanted to tell Andre about Georgia and how I thought she helped me to the top of the silo. The fire began to die down, and Marcel announced we should be on our way.

I could see the Great Stones Ruins glowing in the distance; the lights were leading us back to the Queen. Soon Sager and I would be on our way home. I missed Mommy and Mr. Wienie. I hoped she wasn't worried about us, and I wondered again how long we had been here. Sager was right when she said this world wasn't as it seemed.

We passed by the wagon that still lay on its side stuck in the mud. Geordie jumped from Sager's back to go have a look at what was left behind. I think he was hopeful he would find another jug of carrot cider.

Andre made a funny squeaking noise signaling Marcel that he was going ahead of us. Marcel and Louie were now in the lead. Soon we would be at Resting Flat Rock, where the three trails met each other.

Sager walked beside me. She could tell I was deep in thought; playfully, she nipped at my heels, trying to get my attention.

I was still thinking about Georgia. She couldn't be this monster the elders spoke of to keep children in their beds at night. Her voice was kind and soft, and I was sure she had helped me.

Sager nudged my heels again, and I stopped to look at her. In her eyes, I could see she was thinking about home. She licked my face, and we continued to follow Marcel and Louie.

Looking back at the trail, Sager asked, "I wonder if Geordie found himself another jug of cider?"

As we rounded the corner through the tall grass into the clearing, we arrived at Resting Flat Rock. We could see that Andre was bent over, looking at something.

The closer we got, I could see that it was Stan, and he was babbling Georgia's and Robby's names repeatedly. It was clear from his state of mind that something horrible had happened.

Stan was half-naked and shivering. His eyes were wild with fear; his fur was going in all directions.

Louie knelt down to look into Stan's face. Stan stared at Louie for a moment and then wrapped his arms around his neck.

Andre held out the apron he had gotten back from Robby and assured Stan that he was safe. Stan grabbed his apron and clutched it to his chest, breathing a sigh of relief.

Louie produced a bota bag of fresh water. Stan took a long drink from the bag and started to recall his encounter with Robby. His eyes filled with tears holding his apron to his chest, remembering how they took his things and bullied him.

We all sat to listen when suddenly Geordie burst through the tall, thick grass holding a jug of carrot cider above his head, announcing in a loud voice, "I'm back!" Stan stood up and screamed Georgia's name and tried to hide behind a huge rock.

Geordie was very giggly, and we could tell he had already sampled plenty of the carrot cider.

Andre said, "We are getting nowhere here. I am sure the lookout tower has seen us by now and made the Queen aware of our arrival. We must be going."

Marcel and Louie helped Stan to his feet. Sager flipped a half-drunken Geordie to her back, and I carried the jug.

Halfway up the hill, we could hear the trumpets announcing our arrival. The streets were filling with the well-wishers that had previously watched us leave. They were congratulating and cheering for us once more.

We were escorted back to the great hall, where the Queen sat with Spencer by her side. Marcel and Andre placed the backpacks before her and knelt at her feet to present their swords. One by one, we knelt before the Queen.

In a loud voice, Andre said, "Your Royal Highness, we have returned from The Mighty Hooved One with the bags full of oats as you instructed. How may we be of further service to you?"

The Queen sat quietly as Spencer knelt, opened the backpacks, and tasted the oats. He returned to her side and whispered in her ear.

She rose with a look of approval on her face. As she approached Andre and Marcel, Stan was still babbling and whimpering under his breath.

I could hear Louie trying to make Stan quiet down. Sager wrapped her front leg protectively around Geordie, who was trying not to wobble on his feet.

The Queen handed her scepter to Spencer and placed one front paw on each of Marcel and Andre's heads to gesture a job well done to them. She turned to her Court, raising her arms, she encouraged them to cheer for her Warriors.

The Queen continued to approach us. As she descended the second step, the Queen paused, closed her eyes, and put her nose into the air; she sniffed at Stan and then in my general direction. She stood there in silence as if recalling a memory.

The Queen opened her eyes and motioned to Spencer to stand next to her, only to discover that he was happily pawing through his ever-present bag. The Queen cleared her throat loudly, causing Spencer to jump and move into position beside her. They were both now in front of Louie and Stan.

The Queen's voice became more serious when she asked, "What has happened to this Footman? Who and what is he babbling about?"

Andre rose and said, "Your Highness, if I may?"

The Queen turned to face Andre as he told how Robby and his Band of Bandits had bullied us before leaving The Mighty Hooved One. Andre left out the part about Stan running away because he was frightened by Geordie's tale of Georgia.

The Queen instructed Louie to take Stan back to his station and help him tidy himself, then turned her attention to Sager and me. She asked with a much more condescending tone to her voice, "Have you learned all you needed to know of my Field of Mystery and Wonderment?"

Sager and I looked at each other, unsure which one of us should answer. Impatiently the Queen snapped, "Saver of all Hearts, have you seen all you needed to see in this world of mine?" All the while, the Queen continued to sniff in my direction.

I now knew she was talking to me; I rose and answered yes. As I started to thank her, the Queen sniffed the air even more briskly around me and motioned for Sager to rise. Sager got to her feet, and from the back of the room, we unexpectantly heard Stan painfully scream out Georgia's name.

The Queen's Court burst into a panic, and the room became loud and out of control. Whispers of the myth could be heard from all directions. Spencer returned to the Queen's throne, raising his paw; he tried to be heard over the noise as he demanded order pounding the Queen's scepter on the arm of her throne. The Court blatantly ignored Spencer's order. The words who, who do I feed, who continued to echo throughout the great hall.

Displeased with her entire Court, the Queen returned to her throne and dramatically threw herself down into it with an angry flourish.

Snapping at Spencer, she told him to order the Guard to bring Stan and Louie back in front of her.

Still holding the Queen's scepter, Spencer attempted to pound on the arm of the Queen's throne, not noticing that he missed. The Queen screamed out his name in such a strange way, it made him feel as though he was going to faint.

The air hung thickly as Spencer turned to see the Queen holding her right paw with her left. With a look of contempt that silenced the room, the Queen snatched her scepter away from him; grabbing his arm, she whispered something into his ear.

Spencer nodded his head, showing the Queen he understood her meaning. She now had his full attention. He stepped forward, pointed to the Queen's Guard, and then to my surprise, he pointed at me.

Sager growled as they rudely swooped me up and placed me at the Queen's feet. I could hear Geordie and Andre trying to calm Sager down. She said, "Why is that pudgy skunk sniffing my sister all over?"

The Queen pointed to my collar and held out her paw. Spencer started to fumble with the clasp and then jumped away from me. Gasps of fear were heard from the Court as a dark brown feather slowly floated from my collar to the floor.

Shocked and confused, Spencer stood frozen, looking from the floor to the Queen. The Queen stamped her scepter impatiently and held out her paw, again requesting my collar from Spencer. His whole body trembled as he reached to floor to retrieve the feather.

Spencer turned to the Queen and knew she had not seen it float to the floor. Fearfully he bowed deeply and hesitated, then holding the feather by the tip of its quill; he gingerly held it out to his Queen.

The Queen's eyes began to turn red and bulge, her nose twitched uncontrollably. The whole Court could hear strange squealing sounds coming from the Queen as she bolted from her throne and snatched the feather from Spencer's paw.

The room was in utter chaos. The Queen's Court became frightened, as they had never seen their Queen behaving in such a manner.

Again, the words, who, who do I feed, who were heard amongst the pushing and shoving as the entire Court tried to leave. Enraged even more, the Queen ordered her Guards to take Sager and me to the dungeon.

The last thing I remember seeing was Sager jumping through the air, trying to rescue me.

I awoke to the smell of dirty, musty air. Coughing, I opened my eyes and looked around. I was in a small room with a dirt floor. It was hard to see very far through the darkness. Trembling, I struggled to my feet, and with just a few steps, I discovered; that I was locked in a cage.

Taking a few more steps, I thought I could see Sager lying not far from me. Whimpering, I called Sager's name over and over. "Sager, Sager, are you okay? Wake up, sister, I need you."

Bounding to her feet, Sager let out a growl. Running towards me, I heard what sounded like a heavy chain clanking; suddenly, Sager came to an abrupt halt. I could now see my sister; I gasped and howled loudly. Instantly I realized they had chained my precious sister to a wall.

Sager backed up and repeatedly tried to run towards me. Every time she did, the chain jerked at her neck, making her sit down hard on her haunches. My heart was breaking for my sister; I howled as I watched her, realizing that she was once again locked and chained in a cage.

Feeling hopeless and afraid, it felt like hours had passed, maybe even days; who knew how long we had been locked up. The sun never rose or set here, making time seemingly stand still in this strange little world. Yet it moves so fast beyond our cedar gate.

I was worried that we were never going to make it home. I wondered if Mr. Wienie would come and look for us. I wanted our Mommy and my bed. I started to cry, asking Sager yet again, "Sister, what are we going to do?" Sager's body would only tense and she refused to answer.

As we sat in the dark, I said everything I could think of to convince her not to give up, but I was running out of things to say.

I should have told Sager at the time that I thought Georgia helped me make the long jump to the top of the silo from the old blind horse's back. I wasn't sure at the time it was her, but now I know I am sure.

Sager and I sat waiting in the Queen's jail, but what were we waiting for? My sister was rapidly losing hope; she had stopped trying to free herself from the chain that was around her neck. Then I heard her move, and I strained to see Sager's face in the dark. She was looking at me with tears in her eyes, and barely above a whisper, she said, "I should never have bitten that horse." She closed her eyes, turning away from me. She curled into a tight ball.

At that moment, I felt so much rage towards the Queen. I felt terrible because I promised Sager it would be okay for her to bite Flash; now, I think she thought she was being punished because of it.

Frustrated, I was determined to somehow get to Sager's side. No one, not even a Queen, was going to keep me away from my sister.

I thought if I could get to Sager, I knew I would convince her that it wasn't her fault that we were locked up. Remembering all of the things I am so well known for, I started to dig!

I awoke to Sager licking blood from my feet; I had dug so hard and fast I hadn't even noticed when I injured them. Now I was literally with Sager. I'm not sure how long it took me, and it didn't matter anymore because we were together. I made it!

I started to tell Sager about Georgia when suddenly I could hear Geordie's voice. He was chattering as he looked in on us from a hole in the wall high above. He sounded nervous as he started telling us what had happened after The Queen's Guard took us away. He also asked us question after question but didn't give us a chance to answer.

Looking behind himself, he nodded, then looked back to us and said, "Andre needs Sager's collar."

Before Sager removed her collar, she asked, "Can I keep my charms?" To which Geordie replied, "No, because Andre needs those too. He has devised a plan to set you free from the Queen's dungeon."

I could tell that my sister was worried about losing her charms. I helped Sager take her collar off and watched as she lovingly stroked the one that said, Mommy's Babysitter. Then she tossed the collar to Geordie. It hit the wall just below where Geordie stood and fell to the floor. Geordie reached further into the hole and told Sager to hurry. I watched as Sager snatched up her collar, and with all her might she threw it again, hitting Geordie directly in the face. Geordie said, "Perfect shot! That's my '*bonnie lass.*' " Then he waved Sager's collar above his head in celebration.

We watched as Geordie backed away from the window, telling us he didn't have any more time to explain the plan and promised he and Andre would be back soon to free us.

I was beginning to feel hopeful. Geordie mentioned Andre, but he never said anything about Marcel or even Stan and Louie?

Why do they want to know if our brother, Mr. Wienie is a King or an Emperor? What difference would that make? All of Geordie's questions made me curious, but how was Sager's collar going to help them set us free in any world?

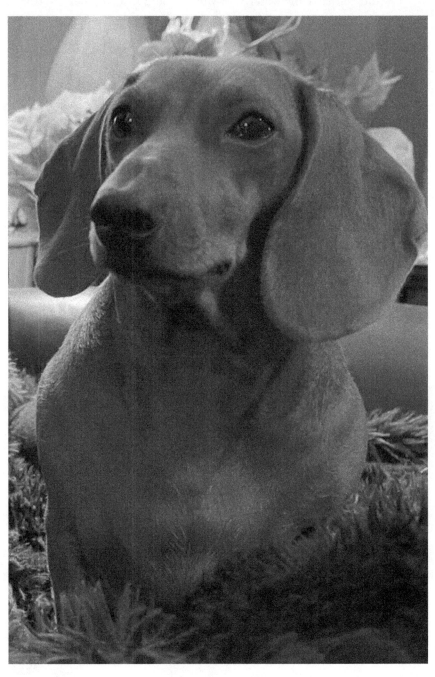

Elizabeth James

ELIZABETH JAMES
Purebred Red Female Dachshund
Born: August 1, 2019

I enjoy playing with toys, digging in the yard, barking, and chasing the neighbor's cat. Favorite indoor past times include but are not limited to racing through the house, greeting guests at the door, collecting items that are not mine, and hiding them in my bed. I seriously can not imagine a life without my Mom, and my sister and brother.

Playtime is a particularly special time for me. It's where I do my most important work with my toys. I'm currently considering creating a series of video tutorials on proper squeaker removal. My brother tells me that if I listen to his suggestions and give him my treats, these video tutorials could win massively in a Drama Series. However, I'm not sure if my brother is referring to my treats or the videos.

Sager Jane

SAGER JANE
Sable Female Chihuahua/Dachshund
(Also known as a Chiweenie)
Born: August 31, 2013

I enjoy playing with toys and pretending that I'm a cattle dog herding cows down a dusty trail. Snapping at every heel from here to the horizon. My Aunt Goldie can personally attest to my swiftness and accuracy.

I am also proficient at getting on the dining room table. I can have a quick bite of food and return to the floor without anyone ever having been aware that I've done so!

My favorite thing ever is to keep my sister and brother from getting into trouble, and I don't care if they think I am a fun sucker! I love to be in charge.

Mr. Wienie

MR. WIENIE
Purebred Black & Tan Male Dachshund
Born: February 2, 2011

I enjoy all things food and being in Grandma's room. She and I spend most days watching television and sharing her snacks, especially when she doesn't know it. I am most passionate about defending the fence line in the yard!

Anytime delivery personnel arrive, I always ensure they are aware of our presence. I feel that this is of the utmost importance to a dachshund of my caliber.

So, back to snacks! Not just any snack will do! It must start and end with the word Bacon. There is no substitute. Because that's how I roll.

ABOUT THE AUTHOR

WENDY J. HATFIELD has found herself fortunate enough these days to spend each day doing exactly as she pleases. Throughout her life, she has never known the meaning of the word quit.

She experienced her share of typical growing pains and everything that went with it. She found everlasting love and lived twenty-nine glorious years of marriage to then be faced with the devastating loss of her husband.

The survivor in Wendy pulled up her bootstraps and went back to the retail workforce as the CEM of Operations for a world-known craft house in her location for 10 years.

Currently, she is retired and enjoys traveling. Her greatest pleasures are spending time with her family and playing with, photographing, and writing about her three beautiful dachshunds, Elizabeth James, Sager Jane, and Mr. Wienie.

CPSIA information can be obtained
at www.ICGtesting.com
Printed in the USA
LVHW031318050222
710024LV00001B/43